Shanta Gokhale was born in Dahanu and brought up in Mumbai. She has worked as a lecturer in English at Elphinstone College and H.R. College of Commerce, as a sub-editor with *Femina*, as a P.R. Executive with Glaxo Laboratories and as arts editor with the *Times of India*. Gokhale has written three novels in Marathi, *Rita Welinkar*, *Tya Varshi* and *Nirmala Patil Yanche Atmakathan*. Two of her novels have won the Maharashtra State Award for the best novel of the year and have been translated by her into English. Her memoir *One Foot on the Ground* was published by Speaking Tiger in 2019. She has translated *Smritichitre: The Memoirs of a Spirited Wife* by Lakshmibai Tilak and the novel *Kautik on Embers* (Dhag) by Uddhav J. Shelke. Apart from these, she has also translated plays by Vijay Tendulkar, Mahesh Elkunchwar, Satish Alekar, G.P. Deshpande, Premanand Gajvi and Makarand Sathe. She has translated from English into Marathi the play *Mister Behram* by Gieve Patel and the novel *Em and the Big Hoom* by Jerry Pinto. She is the author of *Playwright at the Centre: Marathi Drama from 1843 to the Present*; and the editor of *The Scenes We Made: An Oral History of Experimental Theatre in Mumbai*, *Satyadev Dubey: A Fifty-Year Journey Through Theatre* and *The Theatre of Veenapani Chawla: Theory, Practice and Performance*.

She has been a culture columnist with *The Independent*, *The Sunday Times of India*, *Mid-Day* and *Mumbai Mirror*.

She was awarded the Lifetime Achievement Award at Tata Literature Live in 2019, and the Vani Prakashan Award in 2025.

The Way Home

Stories

Shanta Gokhale

SPEAKING TIGER

SPEAKING TIGER BOOKS LLP
125A, Ground Floor, Shahpur Jat, near Asiad Village,
New Delhi 110049

First published by Speaking Tiger Books 2025

ISBN: 978-93-6336-138-6
eISBN: 978-93-6336-900-9

10 9 8 7 6 5 4 3 2 1

Typeset in Minion Pro by SÜRYA, New Delhi
Printed at HT Media Ltd, Greater Noida

Contents

In Remembrance of Times Past

When Nandini walked out of the clubhouse changing room, Ashok's jaw dropped. Perhaps his eyes popped too. I wasn't looking. My eyes were fixed on Nandini as she strode through the lounge waving cheerfully at us, her golf bag slung smartly from her shoulder.

'She's seventy-five?' Ashok asked.

'Same as me. Classmates, as you know.'

'But…'

'Yes,' I said neutrally. 'We are different.'

I was short. I had grown tubby. My hair had gone from a thick glossy braid to a straggly low-hanging ponytail held by a claw-clip. I had been dyeing my hair. Nandini had allowed salt to enter hers. As it grew thinner, she had worn it shorter and shorter till it was a close crew now. The widow's peak still stood out sharply, etched at the exact centre of her hairline pointing down to the top of her delicate nose.

Nandini walked out to the first hole teeing ground, signalling to the caddie for her bag. He sauntered over, not particularly keen to trail an elderly woman over the course. She nodded at him with a brilliant smile, plucked the driver out of the bag, walked to the tee and set her stance.

'She makes a fine figure out there,' Ashok said.

'True,' I said, holding back what would inevitably have followed had I not become weary of saying it. After fifty years together, Ashok and I had only just found the courage to leave the city for this new life in a senior citizens' living facility where everything was laid on, including medical attention, a guest house and a nine-hole golf course. I was making an enormous effort to rid our relationship of the tired tatters of old arguments about what I could have done in life if only…

'She used to wear that outfit when she came back from Stanford and I caddied for her on Sunday mornings at the old club,' I said. I was speaking to nobody in particular. Ashok's eyes had glazed over. 'She is one wealthy woman I know who doesn't discard what is still useful. She carries her mother's frugal blood,' I persisted. Then I fell silent. Umabai Mhatre had been a genius in the kitchen. Her pickles would have made her a pile to equal her husband's. Add her chutneys made from the peel of every known gourd, and she would have been a household name.

Nandini's outfit was a grey divided skirt topped by

a butter-yellow sleeveless polo and a white cap. She had wondered if the skirt would fit. I had said come on, of course it will. She was the only one from our class—of those still living—who hadn't thickened around the waist.

'I hope I don't dig up the turf,' she said when I used golf as a carrot to tempt her to spend the weekend with us. Although she had not played for the last twenty years, she had played for forty years before that. She just had to grab a club now for golf to follow.

It was Nandini's father, Ramchandra Mhatre, who had given her the first lessons in the game. We were in the final year at school. The other girls were abandoning pastimes to plunge full time into school books when Nandini attached herself passionately to ball and club. She tried to teach me too. But I seemed to lack the hand-eye coordination required to bring ball and club together. I gave up in favour of caddying for her. That allowed me the other luxuries of golf—filling my eyes with the deep emerald green of the fairway and my lungs with fresh air. Chembur was not Mumbai's gas chamber then.

Ramchandra lived well. He was the scion of an old landowning Chembur family. Sunday lunch was always at the prestigious Bombay Presidency Golf Club where he was a member. There, picking through the Anglo-Indian menu which Nandini's mother Umabai hated, he would regale us with stories of Chembur as it was when he was growing up. 'Looking down from the top of Trombay Hill, you saw paddy fields and rolling grassland, densely wooded forests and streams running through like silver ribbons. The sea curved around us. We waded into it at low tide and caught large crabs among the rocky shallows. Crabs. Chimborya. Chembur. See the link?'

A series of pantojis would journey from Bombay by train, ferry and train again to home-tutor him. The man who taught him English came dressed in a crisp white dhoti, black jacket, black cap, a cane in hand, pump shoes on feet and an impeccable English accent on his tongue. Unfailingly, as he stepped into the Mhatre courtyard, exhausted by the journey, he would look around at the countryside and sigh, 'A pastoral idyll indeed worthy of the quill of a Keats or a Shelley.'

Unlike other landowners' sons who squandered their inheritance, Ramchandra built on his. He became one of the biggest manufacturers of switches in the country, leaving a thriving business for Nandini and her brother Nachiket to manage after he was gone.

I squinted at Nandini standing poised at the tee with a deeply sceptical caddie looking lazily away as though to say: I have nothing to do with this amateurish tomfoolery. Nandini measured the distance to the pin with her eyes, swung her iron back, down and up in a confident arc that sent the ball to within a metre of the hole. She turned round to us, sitting behind the plate glass of the clubhouse, with a gesture that said I haven't lost it. The caddie woke up, surprised at her immaculate drive and decided to treat her like a man. The first hole was an easy Par 2, but Nandini needed three to hole, having missed it by a whisker on her second putt. I followed her with my eyes till I lost sight of her over a rise. Then I sat back, knowing it would take her a couple of hours to complete the course and get back to us for a drink and lunch.

'Why didn't she marry?' Ashok asked, almost offended.

'She just…didn't.'

'You don't want to say.'

'Why should I not want to say? Let me put it this way. She was too busy to marry.'

'Nobody's too busy to marry.'

'Well, she was. Aah, look here come the Kamaths.'

Omkar Kamath ambled over, ready for the day's argument with Ashok over cricket selections. Saroj followed, shook her head at the two, and settled down to discuss the evening's programme of old film songs that had been laid on for us. We were to hear one of those tiresome singers who did voices. This one was famous for doing Rafi, Mukesh and Talat. Ashok had already said he would come only to hear how this man with a Malayali name would tackle Sahir Ludhianvi and Majrooh Sultanpuri. Having grown up in Indore, he was intensely possessive of Hindi, Hindustani, Urdu, the lot, convinced that nobody south of the Vindhyas should attempt any of them if they did not wish to be charged with murder. In all our years together, I hadn't dared utter a word of Hindi in his presence. Fortunately, given his tours, his presence had been so infrequent that most times I had been free to say kanda-batata to the vegetable vendor instead of aloo-pyaaz. Vegetable vendors from the North are more forgiving than financial advisors from the North.

Nandini was jubilant over lunch. 'Excellent performance,' I said, introducing her to the Kamaths. 'But I'm a little tired,' she said.

After lunch she went to the guest house to rest. When she came down to our room for tea, her glow of good health was back. Her long kurta and palazzos were so perfectly cut, they required no accessories to make them eye-catching. I had made her favourite dish for tea, sabudanyachi khichdi, to which she applied herself with gusto. After polishing off her second helping, she sat back, deeply satisfied, and said, 'Wah!'

Nandini and Ashok had not met more than a couple of times, the first of those times being our wedding fifty years ago. However, they knew enough of each other through me to be tense. Ashok was instinctively uneasy with women of the world and Nandini with men who felt entitled to boss. Caught in that tension, I could neither talk freely nor keep quiet. I chattered non-stop about nothing while they remained silent. It was a relief when tea was done and I could say, 'Let me show you around our glorious hideaway-on-the-hill.'

The walk around the complex was invigorating. At the end, we sat on a bench at a specially created viewing point on the western periphery of the property from where we could see the sun sink behind a distant hill. Below us stretched fields dotted with huts and cottages, and beyond them a stream rippling into the distance. 'Sometimes it is a joy simply to be,' I said. 'To sense, to smell, to see.' I could say that to Nandini and be understood.

As evening darkened into dusk, Nandini turned to me. 'People drink at sundown to keep sad thoughts at bay. This damned nowhere time between day and night brings them on in loads. I don't want to be sad. Let's go.'

'Yes, let's. The music is about to start anyway.'

The singer was a middle-aged man with a severely receding hairline, a perfectly bow-shaped upper lip and melancholic eyes. He was introduced to us as Gopi Nair, a man who had 503 karaoke shows to his credit. We clapped.

'If I have your permission,' the singer began with an obsequious hand-on-heart bow, 'I will begin. I will first sing songs that mean something to me. Then songs that mean something to you. Please put down your farmaish on the slips of paper my assistant will distribute. As you can see, I have titled this programme *Down Memory*

Lane. These are old songs that you grew up with. That we all grew up with.' He laughed self-deprecatingly. But of course, he was a couple of decades younger than the youngest of us.

I was as happy as Nandini to return to the music we had shared as collegians. We had joined a south Bombay college from which Rhythm House had been but a five-minute walk. We often wound up there after lectures to listen to our favourite LPs with no obligation to buy. A boon. I didn't have the money and Nandini's father was moulding her character by not giving her any. When we shared a booth at Rhythm House, we listened avidly to Rafi and Talat alternately. Rafi was my favourite. Talat was Nandini's absolute obsession. But when we managed to get separate booths, she listened to nothing but Talat and I to Kesarbai or Abdul Karim Khan or Bade Ghulam. Every LP was a feast of nine or ten tracks of divine music.

We sat at the end of the fifth row to let Ashok slip away noiselessly when he had had enough. The doors of the mini auditorium were left wide open to let the breeze in. There was much fiddling with the computer on the low stage before we heard the first karaoke track. A collective sigh of recognition went up as the singer hummed the opening notes of that most romantic of numbers, *Chaudhavin ka chand ho*. When the humming gave way to the first words of the song, the audience broke into wonderstruck applause for Gopi

Nair sounded 'exactly like Rafi'. No way, I thought, my hands stiffly apart in my lap. Nair put his hand to his heart, happy to have pleased. As the song proceeded, however, the silliness of the mimicry ceased to matter. The lyrics and the melody took over, drawing us gently into sweet nostalgia. Nandini and I smiled mistily at each other. Ashok leaned over to whisper loudly in my ear, 'Just as I thought. Malayali Hindustani.' He straightened up. Then leaned over again. 'I don't think I'm going to last much longer.'

On the karaoke track, a synthesised sarangi had started to play. Yaman Kalyan, I whispered to Nandini. *Aansu bhari hai*, she whispered back. Nair quickly switched from Rafi's open voice to Mukesh's nasal tone, and once again the audience clapped in amazement. Ashok left. A woman in the row behind us began to sing softly along with Nair. She not only knew the words of *Aansu bhari hai*, but, as it turned out, of every song that followed—*Tasveer teri dil mera behela na sakegi, Khoya khoya chand, Chandan sa badan*—Rafi, Mukesh, Talat and back to Rafi and Mukesh. In the expectant silence that followed, we heard the opening notes of the one song I had hoped Nair would not sing. But there it was, a mish-mash of synthesised notes that were a travesty of Vilayat Khan's superb sitar in the original. Nandini stiffened. As Nair sang *Meri yaad mein tum na ansu bahana,* failing utterly to reproduce the velvet of Talat's voice, she rose and walked out through the side door. I followed.

'That melody, yaar. What is it about those notes that twists the gut?' We were standing under the stars away from the auditorium, leaning against the railings from where the hill sloped down to maize fields.

'That's how Jaunpuri is. Sad and full of yearning.'

'Is it a twilight raag?'

'No. Pre-noon.'

'How? With all that pain and yearning?'

'Pain and yearning, yes, but also resignation. A sad stability.' I looked at her in the over-bright blue of our outdoor lighting. Her face looked pinched.

We sat on a bench, listening to the song as it came over the noiseless air. 'Imagine me all fluttery even now, with the old sadness coming on,' she said, looking at me with a half-smile. 'But it's okay. I don't want to fight it.' She paused. 'The sadness takes me to places in my heart that I don't always have time for.' She paused again. 'It makes me feel fuller. More rounded.'

I was awed to see her like that. To know that she had preserved the pain. Not blunted it with hard logic, with the acceptance of things as they are.

Looking up at the stars etched sharp in an ink-blue sky, Nandini said, 'How much power songs have to bring back a time, a mood, an emotion. The last day of college. Our last visit to Rhythm House. Life was about to change forever. I had listened obsessively to this song, luxuriating in its sadness. You were next door listening to…?'

'Bade Ghulam. *Yaad piya ki aaye.*'

Nair's voice came floating over the silent air. *'Judaa meri manzil, judaa teri rahein / Milegi na ab teri-meri nigahein / Mujhe teri duniya se hai door jaana...'*

'Talat was not singing only about the parting of ways,' Nandini said, her voice low and moist. 'He was singing about eyes destined never to meet again. Never again. That was cruel. A pre-warning of what he...'

We hadn't spoken about him for...I don't know... some fifteen years. Suddenly he was with us. Apurba Bir, the gentle scholar from Odisha, who had asked Nandini for a dance at the college social.

'It's how he led me off the floor,' Nandini had said, sipping tea in the canteen the day after the social. 'His hand on my skin, cool and warm. Both. How could that be? My first time in a sari. My midriff bare. His hand saying: Come. Let's sit and talk.'

They talked the rest of the evening. Then there were daily coffees at the Milk Bar behind the college. They could chat for hours. But they could also be silent, occupied with their own thoughts, yet still together. They were like two streams flowing into one another. I was fascinated. And envious. Ashok was waiting in the wings for me to graduate. My parents were thrilled that his parents had approached them for my hand. He was of our caste. He had excellent prospects. Enough for any young woman to be excited. Even happy.

We emerged from Rhythm House, she full of Talat,

I apprehensive for her. He must be waiting at Wayside Inn next door. Our last day at college. The weight of the occasion lay heavy on both our hearts.

She walked off to the left. I to the right to catch the bus home. She came over late in the evening, her eyes red. He had been there as promised. But silent. It wasn't their usual companionable silence. It was a silence heavy with foreboding. She had felt it. He took her hand in his and told her gently, evenly, about the scholarship he had won to Cambridge. She had expected something else to follow. It hadn't. What had followed, after an unending pause, was this: 'I can make only one promise Piyu. I won't forget.'

'Surely you can write to him?' I was holding her hand tight.

'He hasn't asked me to. He hasn't offered to. It's over. We will never meet.' The tears had flowed freely.

But they did meet in a way. Decades later, he had come on a book tour, Delhi, Calcutta, Bombay. Nandini had attended the launch in Bombay. She had bought the book although she wasn't remotely interested in maritime trade routes in south-east Asia. She had told me lightly of the encounter when it happened; but now she wanted to return to that evening, to relive every detail.

'I had half decided not to go,' she said, her voice low, the late evening breeze causing the tails of her silk scarf to lift and fall on her chest. 'But how could I not push at the aching tooth to feel if it still hurt?' She paused. 'It did, yaar. It did. And how! Forty years and the damned thing still hurt.'

She looked down at her hands lying twined in her lap. Then straight at me. 'I had been with several men. Yes, Saru dear. All over the world. Enjoyed their company. And the sex. But that was nothing compared to the rush I felt listening to Apu talk passionately about those damned trade routes, yaar. It got me up here and down there. It was simple. I wanted him. His voice had deepened. His hair was wispy. He wore reading glasses. But he was still as slim and compact as ever. His sentences too were fashioned like himself. Crisp, unpretentious. And the passion? That was all for the sea, the ships, the enterprise. He made us live the times. He made us see the enormity of the enterprise. My father had been part of that chain. Nachiket and I heirs to it. He was talking about us.'

After a long pause filled with the strains of *Aa laut ke aajaa mere meet* drifting over from the auditorium, she said, 'I stood in the queue waiting to get my copy of the book signed. As the length of the queue decreased, the thumping of my heart increased. It was useless trying to fight it. Memory, anticipation, hope give their own commands to the body. I reached the head of the queue. He held out his hand for the book, his eyes raised. I dared not look at his eyes. I looked at his shoes. "Nandini Mhatre" I said formally, holding the book open at the fly leaf. I didn't want to force him to acknowledge old times. He bent over the book and wrote. I made a grab for the book. He held on to it for just a second longer than he needed to. I looked at him. He smiled. I stumbled down the steps and straight out on to the road and into the car. Sitting in the back seat, I opened the book and flashed my mobile torch on the inscription. It said, "Thank you for coming Piyu. And thank you for buying the book. I hope you will read it. In remembrance of times past. Apu." Hugging the book to my chest, I wept silently. Buckets. Piyu. He remembered the name.'

She shook herself and laughed. 'Mushy, na?'

Aa laut ke aaja mere meet had ended. 'Doesn't this man know any happy songs?' Nandini cried, her voice brassy bright. 'Let's give him our farmaish. *Eena meena deeka*. Come.'

'That's Kishore. He won't sing that.'

'Kishore the sublime madman. Oh well. I guess we are doomed to sadness.'

'No. Listen. Someone else has had the same idea.'

Over the air came Nair's faux Rafi voice singing *Baar baar dekho*. Someone in the auditorium whistled in appreciation. The seniors were returning to old ways.

Nandini stood up. 'Let's dance.'

'No.'

'Yes.'

'No.'

I hadn't danced in six decades. But why not now? Ashok wasn't around with his wet blanket. I rose, giggling stupidly. Nandini grabbed my hand and we flung ourselves into a jive. My feet took off on their own. Dance, like golf, doesn't go away. The air was cold. The wind whipped our faces. We pulled, pushed, kicked and swivelled. My cheeks were getting hot. My eyes began to smart. I was panting. So was Nandini. But nothing could stop us while the song was on. Another two minutes, one minute, thirty seconds, the last second. The farewell chorus, *taali ho* faded into the night. The song stopped. We stopped. We dropped onto the bench, laughing. Laughing loud and long.

Two Men

I turned over. He stood near my bed like Michelangelo's *David*, for God's sake. Difference? Instead of a sling in one hand and a rock in the other, he was holding his tool with both hands.

Of the many questions that sprang to my mind, the most urgent was, 'Why?'

The next one was, 'Do I need to know?'

The third was, 'How should I say "I don't need it" without sounding ungracious?'

I said, 'Are those your clothes, Mohan?'

He said, 'Yes'.

I said, 'Could you put them on, please?'

He said, 'But…'

I said, 'I have seen it. Now it's time to go home.'

His eyes went red with rage. Or some equally strong emotion. I couldn't quite tell in that twilight hour. And my back muscle was still hurting. I switched on the lights.

'Wait,' he said frantically.

'There's no shame now. I've seen it.'

He burst into tears. 'Why are you like that?'

'Like what?'

'Heartless.'

'Did I beat you up with chappals? Did I tell you to get out and never show me your face again?'

He zipped up his jeans, tossed his hair out of his wet eyes and left, banging the door shut.

I opened the door and shouted, 'Your backpack.'

He stormed in, picked up his backpack from the work table and stormed out, banging the door again.

Why had this happened? Had I led him on? Or appeared to have? Jaydeep said I had been leading him on. But that was jealousy. Jaydeep was pathologically jealous of any male who got fond of me. Prof Katre at college for instance. Poor man. He doesn't care for women. He's just a good friend. Jaydeep is unconvinced. There are times when I suspect he is jealous of the very fact of me. What or who I am. Or whatever. I can't plumb his contorted mind. But it affects me more now that I have begun to write plays. He goes most strikingly green when some member of the group likes something I have written. He picks big holes in it. The one who has liked the play argues back for a while, but stops as soon as it becomes clear that Jaydeep is determined not to like the play for no other reason but that he does not want to like it. Few actors will stand their ground too long against a successful director who might offer them a role in his next play. Make Jaydeep unhappy, and he will cast from outside the group. He's done it before.

I have chickened out before myself. You can argue publicly with your husband up to a point. But when the argument threatens to get ugly, you as a wife must step back. Our cave mothers made the rule and it has governed our lives ever since. It is written into our genes. But something has changed inside me with the present play. It is small but powerful. Jaydeep has been dismissive of it as usual. After the first reading, he ground the group down gradually into admitting that perhaps it needed major reworking. I had said I'd give it another look. I needed time to think. Relieved, Jaydeep had felt free to return to discussing a done-to-death play of his choice so that he might do it to death again.

'Classics never die,' he said sententiously. Of course they don't, I thought, my heart hitting hard against my ribcage in anger. If left to themselves. But you, Jaydeep, have strange ideas about classics. You don't go for the really challenging ones. You go for the ones that begin with a bang and end with a whimper. The bang is what you think you are. The whimper is what I know you to be. You don't question. You don't probe. You accept. Then you proceed to decorate the play. You are perfect for the commercial stage where you are king. Bold idea, cop-out end and gimmickry. The true classic doesn't need decoration or gimmicks, Jaydeep. It stands on the strength of its ideas, its rhythm, its flow, its language. You can play it on bare boards and still hold the audience captive.

I was building up my courage to stand up for my work. I had said I'd take another look. Jaydeep had shrugged as if to say, it's your funeral. It wasn't. It was going to be his. I was planning to play the shirt trick on him. Years ago, he had liked a shirt in a shop and tried it on. It looked fine to me and the shop assistant. But Jaydeep had to find fault. He decided it was too tight under the arms. The counter assistant said, our tailor will fix it. How, Jaydeep demanded. It's a readymade shirt. Doesn't stop our tailor from fixing it, grinned the man. He took the shirt away and was back in ten minutes, smiling. Done, he said, holding out the shirt, now a little crumpled. Jaydeep tried it on. Thanks, he smiled, pleased with himself. Perfect fit.

Back home that evening, I sat at my work table for two days with Jaydeep's suspicious eyes on me. I frowned, looked into space, tapped on my laptop keys urgently, looked out of the window thoughtfully. On the second day, evening, I sat back with a sigh of satisfaction. 'Done,' I said.

I read out the play again to the group. Some of them realized what I had done. Or not done. I caught sly smiles. Jaydeep did not, not because he was dumb but because he was blind with rage. He had barely bothered to listen to the play the first time around and was giving it the same treatment again. He was hardly going to notice that this tailor had done nothing with the tight armhole.

As soon as I was through, Jaydeep began to list objections with pretended critical objectivity. The group wanted no trouble. They wanted roles. They went along with him.

'Wasn't there a film called *Bheja Fry*?'

'Oh yes,' chorused the group.

'We'll have to change the title.'

'Done,' I said. 'It is now *Bheja Double Fry*.'

The group laughed. Jaydeep produced a thin-lipped smile.

'Jokes apart,' he said, 'What do you people think of the protagonist? Doth she not protest too much?'

Actors are not in the habit of reading. Least of all Shakespeare. Being on stage is the thing. They looked at Jaydeep blankly. Jaydeep loved that.

'*Hamlet*? Shakespeare's *Hamlet*?'

The group laughed sheepishly. 'Yes, of course, sir.'

'Good. So, Hamlet asks his mother Gertrude how she likes the play that they are watching. You know, don't you, that there is a play within a play in *Hamlet*? Remember Hamlet says, "The play's the thing /wherein I'll catch the conscience of the king"?'

The group nodded uncertainly.

'Gertrude's answer to Hamlet is, "The lady doth protest too much, methinks." What she means is that the character she refers to as the lady, speaks too long and too volubly of her love and fidelity thereby losing credibility.'

'What Jaydeep is saying,' I pointed out helpfully, 'is that by allowing my protagonist to speak her mind without mincing words, I have made it difficult for you to believe in her. Let me ask you a simple question. Do you find my Sita believable? Or not?'

The silence that followed was unpromising. Then Shikha spoke up. She knew she would be cast as Sita. As an actor, whether the character was believable or not did not matter. She wanted desperately to put her tongue to the last speech.

'She is totally believable,' she declared with conviction, avoiding Jaydeep's eyes.

Avantika who knew she would not be cast for the role said, 'I don't know. I guess most of us would not say the things she says to her husband. I know I wouldn't. I would put it more subtly. My mother always says wives should not give in to their husbands, but wait for the right moment. They should sweeten them first, then tell them off gently. This one simply blows her top.' Avantika's mother was an inescapable presence in group discussions.

There was silence. Jaydeep looked around democratically.

Mohan said, 'I think Sita is a great character. I support strong women. Women have been suppressed for far too long. They must speak up.' Some of the group tittered. Mohan blushed. His voice rose. 'I know what philandering husbands think. What is a one-night stand? A marriage is a marriage. Where will she go? Sita's husband is one of those.'

'My objection is to the name,' Veer said, ignoring Mohan. His voice had a distinct edge.

'But I'm changing it to *Bheja Double Fry*, Veer,' I said.

'I mean Sita. Why Sita? There are many other names. You shouldn't hurt our sentiments.'

'I agree,' Om said. 'Your Sita's language is not the language Sita should use.'

'Let's not go to the epics,' I retorted. 'Sita is a common name. My Sita has nothing to do with the epic Sita. The epic Ram was revered for his fidelity to his wife. My Dheeraj cheats on his. The question here is, is my Sita credible as a modern woman or not?'

Jaydeep sighed. 'Perhaps I started with the wrong observation. This discussion has gone nowhere. And yet we must admit that the majority here is uncertain about your protagonist, Ashwini. Since she is the absolute centre of your play, perhaps we should give you another chance to rethink and rewrite.'

I stood up. My tongue felt heavy in my mouth. My hands were damp. My legs had turned to jelly. These signs said that I had had enough. I was going to speak up and to hell with what our cave mothers taught us.

'No,' I said. A tremor shook my voice. 'I will not rethink. I will not rewrite. This is my third draft. I am satisfied with it.' I turned to Jaydeep. 'All I want to know is, are you going to direct it as it is or not?'

'I will if you insist,' he conceded, keen to preserve his democratic image. 'As long as you allow me to change things where I think they aren't working.'

'Not unilaterally. We will discuss what you think is not working and if I agree it isn't, I will make the changes.'

Jaydeep sighed. Looking around at the actors' embarrassed faces he said quietly, 'Don't you think we could discuss this in private, Ashwini?'

'No, I don't. This is a play. Not a pregnancy.'

Jaydeep sighed again and gave the actors another look that said, you see how it is? The actors squirmed.

'And anyway, you always say the group is family.' I paused, waiting for him to pick that up. He didn't.

'You always say we are family, so nothing should be private.' My tone remained unchanged, but the tremor in my voice had disappeared.

Jaydeep's home face now came on. 'Don't be literal.'

'Aren't we family then? I want clarity.'

'Okay. We are. Now can you lower your voice?'

'No, I can't. Let me go back to repeating what I said. I will not allow you to tamper with the play unless you convince me it needs changing.'

'This was something we discussed when we decided

to marry. A director marrying an aspiring writer can get messy, I said. And you…'

'I know what I said. I said, not if there is mutual trust and respect.'

'And the way to achieve that was to divide our work. I would direct and you would do the research and costumes, not meddle with my work.'

'Then I grew up by a natural process, Jaydeep. I learned what theatre could be. I have written two plays before this. You rejected both.'

'Did we not agree democratically that they didn't work?'

'I liked them,' Mohan said. 'They were good. They worked for me.'

'Your opinion doesn't count. You are her chamcha.' Jaydeep's voice was ice.

'May I suggest the others are yours?' I retorted.

'That's not fair,' Veer said. 'We agreed that your plays were too much about women. Women are free today. Why should they shout so much?'

'Veer,' my voice was suddenly gentle. 'Is that why you are so keen to do *Sarita*?'

'You are dead right. Sarita knows how the cards are stacked against women. But she doesn't lose her dignity by shouting.'

'No. She picks up her drunken, self-centred, domineering husband's shoes at the end of her learning process. That I suppose is the most dignified thing for a human being to do…'

'She sees how shattered he is. That's love. That's understanding. Isn't that what you said, sir, when this one raised a question about the end?'

Veer looked at Kshitija who was staring out of the window. Now she muttered, 'I didn't agree.'

'With what?' Jaydeep asked, his lips thinning.

'With what you said, sir. About love and understanding and dignity.'

'You didn't say it then.'

'I was new. My opinion didn't count. Still doesn't.'

Jaydeep rose. 'I don't think there's anything more to be said. Hands up those who think *Bheja Fry* doesn't work.' Three hands went up with conviction. Two went up halfway. Two stayed down. Irritated Jaydeep said, 'Hands up those who think *Sarita* works.' All hands shot up except the two that had stayed down.

'That settles it. We do *Sarita*. Those who don't think it works are free to opt out. It's a tough play. Raw realism. A woman sold in a bazaar. More feminist than anything a card-carrying feminist could write. We'll meet tomorrow for another reading.'

Jaydeep collected his stuff. 'I'm going to Shekhar's place to discuss the set,' he said to me over his shoulder. 'I'm not home for dinner.'

'Neither am I,' I said. Jaydeep heard me. Must have. But pretended not to and walked off.

'What will you do now, ma'am?' Kshitija said.

I looked hard at her. 'I will direct the play myself. You will play Sita.'

'I can't. I...'

'You can. I'll make sure you can.'

'What about me?' Mohan asked.

'You'll play the philandering husband, of course,' I grinned.

'But he is macho. I'm not...'

'I think you are, dear. Macho is a state of mind, not body. And you're not coming home with me today. I can carry my own bag. Anyway, I'm not going home.'

'Not going home?'

'No. I'm going to Chowpatty.' I looked at Mohan's face and laughed. 'Don't look so worried. I don't plan to walk into the water. I plan to sit on the sand and stuff my face with bhelpuri and sev puri.'

I don't get her. Like she didn't get me.

Macho! A state of mind. She thinks my state of mind is macho. What's wrong with her? Can she not see? Can she really not see that my state of mind is just one thing. Adoration of her.

It's been a shit life. From school on.

She was different. I thought she understood. Wrong. Turns out she didn't.

What did I do? There's a word in her play. Introspect. It's to examine your ideas, thoughts and feelings. I know what mine are. I can reel them off. I have been examining them from when they first called me girlie at school. They said show us you're a boy. They came to the washroom with me.

Then they said, 'You're not a boy. You don't play football.'

I said, 'You don't paint. I paint.'

'Girlie,' they said.

There are no girlie painters. All painters are men. The great ones. The Old Masters. Football! They know nothing. Idiots.

Then our voices broke. I let my beard grow. It was thick and strong.

'Gays too have beards,' they said.

How do you show you are not gay? How do you show what you are not? You can only show what you are.

At college I played Hamlet. My legs looked good in tights. My body looked good in a tunic. I was happy. I had found my world. Theatre. That's how I met Ma'am. She taught us English. She directed *Hamlet*. I fell in love with her. Madly in love. I loved the way she walked, talked, dressed. I watched her through the day. I fantasized about her at night. But she had her Jaydeep. He was from drama school. She invited him to direct *Woyzek* for the college. I was Woyzek. I didn't like the character. He was a loser. He allowed things to happen to him. He was helpless against exploitation, helpless against humiliation. I knew the character inside out. It depressed me to play him.

What I couldn't forgive him for was the end. He killed the woman he loved, with whom he had lived for years, with whom he had had a baby. He should have killed the man, the handsome drum major with whom he had caught her sleeping. I would kill Jaydeep Sir any day I found him hurting Ma'am.

He was mean to her during rehearsals. Once they fought and he shouted, 'Don't interfere with my work' in front of us. She walked away, wounded. I forgot my lines that day, I was so upset. That night I thought of killing him. I slipped out of the house, prowled around their house saying, 'I will kill you, you bastard.' But I had nothing to kill him with. No knife. No stone. Just a thought. Suddenly I was sweating. I went home. Was that a macho state of mind?

But there are other things people like me can do. I would be her protector. Fill in the blanks of her life. If he hurt her, I would soothe her with balm. That would be my mission. Filling in the blanks.

These are my ideas, my thoughts, my feelings. That is what introspection has revealed to me. Introspection is also supposed to lead to understanding. I must understand why I did what I did that evening. We had been rehearsing in her flat. It was cramped, now that the door between the two flats was kept locked on both sides—the fallout of the showdown. Kshitija had left. I was helping Ma'am bring the chairs, the beanbag, the floor mattress, cushions and stuff out of the bedroom into the sitting room.

I remember saying to Ma'am in passing, 'Avantika is living with him.'

'Him?'

'Jaydeep Sir.'

'Good for him. He couldn't have managed on his own.'

'She's playing the main role in *Sarita*.'

Ma'am perched herself on the edge of a chair.

'That's not the main role. The main role is the husband. The father. Kamala, the village woman who gets sold in the bazaar and opens that namby-pamby wife's eyes to what being a woman means. Kamala knows how the cookie crumbles. I suppose Shikha is playing her.'

'She is…Do you miss him?'

'Him?'

'Jaydeep Sir.'

'Do I? Let me think. Actually…no. Not in a way that makes me unhappy. In a way that makes me happy.'

'Happy?'

'When I'm deeply immersed in my writing and nobody is hovering around me impatiently saying, "I was waiting to tell you…" Times like that.' She got off the edge of the chair and walked into the bedroom to shift a thing or two more.

I hadn't said the real thing that was in my mind when I asked her if she missed him. I had meant as a man. Did she miss Jaydeep Sir as a man? You don't spell out these things. You are supposed to read signals. I thought she had read the signal.

I had told her to leave the heavy shifting to me. I took the last chair out and came back for the mattress. She must have tried picking it up. I saw it half rolled and she standing with her hand to her back, her face screwed up in pain. I felt a stab in my heart to see her like that. I rushed to her. I took her hand. Lay her down on her bed.

'It's nothing,' she said. 'Pulled a muscle, that's all. I'll be fine. Can you open that drawer please?'

I opened the drawer.

'Do you see a tube of Volini?'

There it was.

'Bring it here. I can't get to the muscle. You'll have to help me.'

I helped her turn over. Every move made her wince.

'Just pull up my top please. Run your hand along my waist.'

I had never touched her before. I mean I had never ever touched her before in real life. I had to do it now. It was a clear signal. My hand trembled as I ran it over her waist. I could see the bottom edge of her bra.

'Yes there,' she said.

I put a blob of ointment on the spot and began to rub it in gently.

'Ah,' she said. 'That feels good. You have gentle hands, Mohan.'

Her voice came out husky. That was the second signal. My body was doing things.

'Enough,' she said. I stopped. She lay there, her midriff bare.

Then a thought struck me. Perhaps those signals were not what I thought they were. Perhaps she thinks what others have thought. Why else would she allow me to touch her so intimately? Perhaps she feels safe with me. Well she is safe, but not in this way. I must be bolder. Subtle signals won't do.

I felt nothing about dropping my pants. I had done it often enough in my dreams. She turned over. She looked at me. Her eyes grew wide. Then she said what she said. I felt humiliated. Enraged. Hurt. I wasn't showing off. I was offering her my love. If she didn't want it, she could have slapped me. As hard as she wished. She had the right. But she didn't. She bypassed the whole thing. She handled me. Yes, she handled me. And bundled me out.

Kshitija called last week. 'What happened? Why haven't you been coming for rehearsals?'

'Hasn't Ma'am told you?'

'No.'

'Nothing?'

'No. What?'

'That I'm not well?'

'No.'

'So, what has she said?'

'She says: Give him time. He'll come.'

'She does, does she?'

'What more can she say? You know how she is. So understanding. Look. It's pointless rehearsing by myself. When are you coming?'

'As soon as I'm better.'

It took me a week to feel better. I love the role I am playing. I love the end when Dheeraj gets his comeuppance.

I walk into the flat as usual. Ma'am smiles at me as usual. We rehearse as usual. We have tea and biscuits as usual. Ma'am says, 'You were very good today, Mohan. Wasn't he, Kshiti?'

'He was. You should fall ill more often.' Kshitija laughs.

Ma'am does not laugh. I think she understands that I would feel very hurt if she did.

I ring the bell of her flat and wait. No answer. She's probably in the shower. I return to my flat. I pace the floor. Something's wrong in my head. Something's going on there that I can't understand. Who was wrong? Was it such a big thing that we had to separate?

It became big. It was made big. A director must feel excited by a play. He can't direct if he doesn't see it unfolding before his eyes. He must be able to own it.

This play of Ashwini's…it did nothing for me. Nothing. None of her plays do. That's the truth of it.

A director is not…a director has to be…the captain of the ship. Without him the ship loses direction. That's simple to understand. Nothing difficult there. There can't be order if we don't want order. If we want order, we must believe in the system that ensures it. She mustn't interfere with my authority as director. I don't interfere with her authority as costume designer. I must make her see reason. She must see that breaking up like this makes her the loser. The world is full of wonderful plays that I want to direct. I have producers to back me. I have made a place for myself in the theatre industry. She is a newbie. She is directing her first play. I admire her guts. But guts aren't enough. You need a stage. You need funds. Which producer will back her? If I and a majority of my actors have rejected her play…if we found the protagonist unacceptable—will our producers think differently? Or our audiences?

Even then, I'm prepared to back her. She will need my backing. I know people on the circuit. I know the ropes. I'll handle them for her. It's an unbeatable offer. She'd be mad not to accept it.

She must be out of the shower.

I ring the doorbell of her flat. I hear sounds. She opens the door.

'Oh hello,' she says.

'Hi!' I reply. I flop onto the beanbag and sink in. She stands before me.

'Won't you sit?' I ask.

'Sure. If I can have my beanbag.'

I get up and move to the mattress.

'What are you cooking this evening? I thought I'd drop by for a bite.'

'Cooking? I don't cook.'

'How do you eat then?'

'I order a dabba.'

'What? But you're such a bloody good cook. Cordon Bleu standard.'

'I know. But I'm also a bloody good writer.'

Oh! The ego of the woman!

'Where do you get your dabba from?'

'I'll give you the address and phone number. It's nothing fancy, mind. Just the regular chapati, veg and dal.'

'I wasn't asking for myself. I'm managing.'

'Oh of course. Avantika.'

'Nonsense. She gets me food occasionally. That's all.'

'I'm happy for you.'

I need to get to what I came to say quickly before she starts an argument. I shouldn't have started on food.

'We don't have to be like this, do we? After fifteen years?'

'You mean independent?'

'You know I don't mean that.'

'True. But that's what I mean. Aren't you enjoying your independence? I am. I'm working on another play.'

'Really? Good. I mean great. I wish the mainstream stage was open to your kind of play.'

'I don't want to be on the mainstream. I don't need to make a living off theatre. I love teaching.'

'So what's the point of writing plays? Where will you go with them? That's why I'm here. Your *Bheja Fry*. It has elements that might go down well with a producer I know. I could put in a word for you. Help you along. Just an offer. You are rehearsing hard. I know. But you will need to perform somewhere. Where, is the question.'

'In people's homes. It has been done before. '

'By men. Women haven't done it and shouldn't. Too risky. You never know.'

'Oh come on. It can't be as risky as climbing Everest. Junko Tabei did it when she was forty-four. I'm only trying to stage a play.'

'She must have been a trained mountaineer. This is your first attempt at direction.'

'Trained or not trained she once said in an interview that most Japanese men of her generation thought she would do better to stay at home and clean house.'

'Well, if you insist on making life difficult for yourself, who am I to stop you?'

With her I know when it is time to give up.

'But my offer holds. Anytime you want to take advantage of it, just knock on my door.'

'You're really sweet, Jaydeep. I mean that's really,

really kind of you. Particularly after the things I said that evening.'

'Oh I don't hold any of that against you. One says these things in anger.'

'True. I was angry. Very angry. But...'

'But what?'

'But I am not retracting any of them.' She grins.

'Come on. Don't bring your ego into this. You're only hurting yourself if you do.'

'Hell. You really don't get it, do you? This isn't ego. This is self-respect. What I'm trying to say is, if I spoke in anger that evening, it wasn't a sudden flare-up. I said what I did because I'd been saying it to you silently for years.'

There's a ring at the door. She gets up quickly to open it. Someone passes a glass of tea to her.

'*Aur ek dena, bhai*,' she says.

She turns with a glass of tea in each hand. She kicks the door shut behind her and holds out a glass to me.

'Good strong brew,' she says. 'Home delivery. You should drop in at this time while my college is on vacation. We can sip tea together and chat about theatre. I was reading this amazing play, *The Jungle*. It's about a refugee camp. Raw. Partly structured, partly spontaneous...'

'We should do that.'

'What?'

'Meet and talk about theatre one of these days. I must go now.'

I rise. So does she, preceding me to the door.

'The offer is still open,' I say, turning to face her.

'So is mine. If Avantika doesn't work out.'

That's not the way I had wanted it to go. Damn her.

The Quilt

While every other woman she knows wears her hair short, Mugdha has never stepped inside a beauty salon to have hers cut. It hangs like a serpent down her back, ending below her buttocks in a long tuft clasped by a black band. Her thick eyebrows run straight over her eyes and angle down sharply at the corners. Her deep black eyes twinkle below them when she is amused and smoulder when she is angry. The heat then is so intense, that you feel singed if you are standing in the direct line of her gaze. She is not a large woman. Rather small in fact. But her shoulders are strong and her back erect, giving her the appearance of stature.

That erect back is now sending signals to her to stop work. She sighs and rolls up the half-made quilt. She pulls her workbox towards her and places in it squares and triangles of multi-coloured fabric pinned together carefully and marked with a number, so she knows which stack goes into which row of the patchwork pattern she has designed. She is not a dedicated quilter; but during a field trip she had made to Chikhali village with her mother, she had watched the women work laboriously on their vakals. They had wanted no truck with her mother's NGO and the new patterns it offered that would make their traditional skills saleable in urban centres.

Like the Chikhali women, she too uses thick cotton thread and a pack needle to quilt. Like them she sits on the floor to work. Like them, she allows the backing to pucker and puff between rows of stitching, making her quilt look softer and warmer than the manicured American quilts she has seen. But, unlike the women who hold age-old patterns in their heads, she has drawn hers on graph paper and measured her fabric with a measuring tape, not by span-length and finger-width. Sitting in the spacious living room of her old family home in south Bombay, she feels the same visceral connection with the quilt taking shape under her fingers that she imagines Janakibai must have felt for her quilts. No wonder she was reluctant to part with even one to Mugdha's mother.

Janakibai was a tall woman with a high forehead marked by a large round spot of vermilion. She had made many excuses not to display her quilts before Mugdha's mother and her assistant. When she was finally persuaded to show them, Mugdha's mother had fallen in love with one. Janakibai had used an old midnight blue sari for it. On it were sewn strips of multi-coloured fabric in concentric circles from edge to centre where they ended in an orange circle, a radiant sun, holding the whole pattern together. Mugdha was spellbound.

'Give me this piece,' her mother had said. 'It will fetch you a good price. A very good price.' Janakibai had given her an icy look instead, stood up and walked away, the quilt clutched close to her chest. Savitribai who was taking the group around, said, 'That one will never sell. Too proud. They are her children she says. As though ours are orphans.'

Mugdha understands that intimate connection now. She understands why she has instinctively chosen the maroon silk sari she had worn on her first date with Vijay as backing.

'I'm so happy you wear saris,' he had said, unable to take his eyes off her. 'And that lovely long plait.'

Her childhood friend Sundar's boyfriend had pestered her to wear jeans.

'You look like an aunty in saris,' he had said. Sundar had taken to jeans to please him. Then he had dropped Sundar for Shubhangi. Sundar had moped till her family had hitched her up with Anand who loved saris because they were Indian and made a woman look graceful and, well, like a woman for heaven's sake. Sundar who was now comfortable in jeans, arrived at a compromise with

Anand. Jeans when I go out on my own; saris when I come out with you.

Mugdha lives alone not too far from Vijay's office. It has become a habit for him to stop by for a cup of tea, hot snacks and intimacy before he proceeds home. This kind of privacy is beyond dreams in Bombay. Nobody around to inhibit their love-making except for the occasional crow on the parapet of the terrace, and unfortunately, beyond a point, Mugdha's morals.

Once on a rainy evening, early on in their romance, he had described his fantasy to her. It is their wedding night. They are in their bedroom, she in her silks and gold, he in his brocade sherwani. She sheds her silk and her gold bit by bit till she is left with only her long, loose hair to cover herself with. He pushes the black cascade away and...

He did not know it, but Mugdha's heart had thumped at the idea. And yet when he suggested in a whisper that they could easily fulfil his fantasy before the first night, her mind had stayed firm. 'This place, this season, they are so perfect. Come on Mugdha,' he had said. But she had refused to come on.

'Are you living in the last century?' he had asked angrily before giving up trying to seduce her.

'Perhaps,' she answered. 'Ajji did and she was...'

'Oh God, your grandmother again. Yes, I know she brought you up because your mother was never there and you loved and admired her. But everything in its proper place please. She can't stand between you and me every time I...'

Mugdha's eyes had looked straight into his as he spoke and what he was saying now sounded...well, just wrong. When she answered him, her voice had been firm.

'Ajji gave me one mantra for life. Do what you think is right. Not what someone else thinks is right.'

'Oh? So now I'm someone else. That's fine. It's good to know where I stand. But that mantra is bad for you. It makes you rigid. If you don't bend, you'll break.'

'It has not made me rigid because Ajji added a rider to it. Think deeply and seriously about what others say. If you think they are right, don't let your ego stand in the way. Give in.'

'So, you've thought seriously and deeply...'

'Yes, I have.'

'And yet...?'

'And yet.'

'Where does that leave love?'

'You mean love as in making love?'

'I mean making love as the ultimate expression of love.'

'Till then love doesn't exist?'

'Of course it does. You always catch me out in words.'

'I always try and understand what your words mean.'

Vijay had rolled his eyes, shrugged and sulked.

Mugdha walks out on to the terrace, pulling herself up and straightening her shoulders. Her barrister great-grandfather had bought this house in Girgaon, the south Bombay locality where the first settlers from the coast had arrived looking for education and work. The family's living quarters had occupied the second and third floors, great grandpa's office the first, and a restaurant that served homely food to working men living away from their families, the ground floor. The spacious, high-ceilinged rooms of the family quarters with their well-oiled timber beams and tiled roof, had once been filled to bursting with uncles, aunts, children and dependents. Gradually the family had dwindled, till, as Mugdha remembered it growing up, it had been reduced to Granny, an old live-in domestic, an even older cook who was going blind, a retired father who spent his time reading philosophy and a generally absent social worker mother.

Now Mugdha is alone.

She leans against the parapet looking down at the narrow, crowded street, enjoying the breeze that has begun to blow from the Arabian Sea in the afternoon. Turning away, she spreads a mat on the mosaic tiles of the terrace. With only a crow on the parapet as witness, she begins to do yoga. Half-an-hour later, she is on her back in shavasana, the corpse pose. The goal of the asana is to bring body and mind together in equilibrium with each other and with the world. But it is not happening. Vijay's visits of late have been tense. He has been distracted, not really enjoying the tea or the snacks or her company.

'Something worrying you?' she asked him at last, taking his hand and holding it in both of hers.

'Why should there be?'

'I don't know. Boss trouble?'

'I've told you I can manage him.'

'Something else then?'

'Will you get off my back? If you're going to nag me like this I…'

She was hurt. She said nothing. He said nothing. They parted coldly. She spent the night wondering what had happened all of a sudden. Light dawned with dawn. He was finally gearing up to tell his mother about them. If they were to marry in December as they had planned, he needed to tell her now. His mother was a die-hard believer in caste. As a brahmin, she had an ill-disguised contempt for those who were not. Mugdha was not. Vijay had assured her he would manage his mother. But perhaps she was not as easy to manage as his boss was. If only he would tell her what was happening. Instead, there was the phone call yesterday.

'Hey Mugdha, I can't come over this evening. The office is sending me out on work for a week.'

'But that's tomorrow or later. You can come today, can't you? I've sprouted beans for misal.'

'Can't Mugdha. Can't. I'm expected to make a presentation. Must prepare for it. And then packing and all that.'

Mugdha was confused. 'I understand,' she said uncertainly.

But she did not. He was not in the kind of job where he would get sent out suddenly for a whole week. Expected to make a presentation? To whom? For what? He was lying.

'Hey, are you there? Don't be like that. I'll call every night. Promise.'

Mugdha decided to believe him.

'I'm glad we aren't meeting Vij,' she said without conviction. She was a bad liar. 'I will have time to finish this beautiful thing. Our quilt.'

'Don't talk about that quilt to me. You're more wrapped up in it than in me.'

They laughed.

Vijay had never been too keen on the quilt. It gave her a joy that he was not part of. She showed him her design, discussed the fabric colours with him, told him of a new technique she had invented to get the puckers she wanted without the backing or the batting or the fronting extending beyond each other. The only thing she didn't tell him was the sari she had picked for the backing. That was her secret.

'Why put so much time and effort into this thing? You'll spoil those beautiful eyes,' he said once. Another time it was, 'When are we going to need this thing? Do we have anything that can be called winter in this city?'

'We do,' she had answered, laughing. 'At least I do. January and February are winter. They follow the month of our wedding. That's when we will use it.'

'You call that winter?' he had shrugged. 'But we can always use it as a bedspread.'

'No, we will not. We will sleep under it.' Then, with a mischievous twinkle in her eyes she had said, 'Your mother wants grandchildren, doesn't she? Well, she shall have them. We'll make one every winter.'

That thought stirred him. He took her in his arms and seemed on the point of starting the process there and then, when she had withdrawn, most reluctantly.

The quilt is done. Vijay is back, but has not come over.

'I'll show it to you when you come tomorrow evening,' she says when he calls.

There is silence at the other end. Then, 'I might not be able to come. There will be a load of backlog to get through at the office. But I'll come in a couple of days. Promise.'

Sundar comes to see the quilt.

'It is special, really special,' she says. 'Vijay will love it when he sees it.'

'I hope so.'

'Why hope?'

'I don't know.'

Sundar is more like a sister than a friend. She is going to be her karavali.

'Don't be silly,' she said when Mugdha told her. 'You know me. I hate rituals. I'll feel like a fool standing behind you with a waterpot and a coconut.'

'But you will kindly agree to look like a fool. I don't have a sister. I have only you.'

Sundar had sighed. Now she says, 'I don't like it.'

'Like what?'

'That Vijay hasn't seen this work of art yet.'

'It isn't going away. It's made to last fifty years. My daughter will make her babies under it!'

'So why hasn't he seen it? Not when you were working on it. Not now that it is done. Why? Don't tell me. Let me guess. Too much work at the office?'

Mugdha goes suddenly silent. Sundar hugs her. 'Trust me to say the wrong thing. He'll come, yaar. He was never too excited about the quilt, was he?'

'No, he wasn't.' That breaks through Mugdha's gloom and they begin to chat about Sundar's promotion which should have come by now and hasn't.

'I tell you. That Vengsarkar has it in for me…'

Sundar leaves well after sundown.

'Look Vijay,' Mugdha says, the evening Vijay finally turns up. There has been a quick, brisk shower a little earlier and it is pleasant on the terrace with the fresh breeze drying their sweaty May bodies. 'You've been sitting there talking about things that don't matter.

There's something on your mind. The sooner you tell me what it is, the lighter you'll feel. Is it the boss?'

Vijay looks at his fingernails and says, 'No. It is something else. I don't know how to tell you.'

Mugdha remembers the implication of Sundar's question, and a large ball of something heavy plummets from the region of her heart to the region of her stomach.

Vijay looks at her. 'You've guessed, haven't you?'

'You've found someone else.' Mugdha's voice is leaden.

Vijay laughs nervously. 'No, no. Not that. There can't be anyone else. But…'

'But what?' Mugdha's eyes are beginning to burn. She looks directly at Vijay from under her straight eyebrows.

'It's Aai. She isn't having it.'

'I see. And what are you planning to do about it?'

'What can I do? You know how she is.'

'No, I don't. You tell me.'

'She insists I see other girls.'

There is a long pause while Mugdha looks straight at Vijay and Vijay avoids looking straight at her. Then she says in a steely voice, hoping against hope that she has got it wrong, 'If you've been seeing girls and your mother has chosen one and you have liked her and it is all fixed and the wedding is to be in December, you just have to say yes and I'll try to understand.'

Vijay doesn't say yes; but every muscle in his face says it.

Mugdha goes to Bordi, leaving her cell phone behind but carrying books. For seven days she reads herself into other worlds. For seven nights she adds her salt to the sea rumbling across the sand from the cottage she is staying in. This is one of four built on the beach for alumni's family and friends by the residential school where her father was sent to save him from being spoilt by his mother. For seven mornings she walks among the casuarinas on the beach, talking to herself. There is not another soul around. Only the old caretaker who says every night before she goes to bed, 'Tai, don't be afraid. I will sleep on the verandah.'

If there is one thing Mugdha has rarely felt, it is fear.

When Mugdha hears Vijay's voice saying hello on the phone, she is aghast. She does not say hello back.

'I know you're wondering why…' he stammers. 'Let me come and explain. Please. We've broken up but we aren't enemies, are we? At least not from my side.'

She utters her first words. 'You mean you have a side?'

'Look, Mugdha, I know you are hurt…'

'I want to end this conversation. I don't want to see you. Period.'

Those words are final. Or so she thinks. They are not. He calls again, then twice more the next day. You have to pity a man like that. She pities him. 'Don't come. Just tell me what you want.'

'I want to say sorry.'

'Try again. You might get to the truth.'

'You're very harsh.'

'That's right. I am.'

There is a long silence at the other end. 'This is very awkward.'

'Truth is.'

'No. Talking over the phone. On a sensitive issue.'

'Not my problem.'

'You refuse to forgive? I am desperate for you to forgive me. I have destroyed your life...'

'You haven't. My life isn't so fragile. And I don't remember having handed it over to you.'

'All right. You win. Can I write to you?'

'If you must. Makes no difference to me either way.'

When the letter comes, she is even more aghast.

My dearest friend Mugdha,

'I will confess to you, because you have always been generous in your understanding of me, that all is not well between Avantika and me. She has got wind of us. I mean what there was between us. I must confess that I had asked Aai very tentatively how she would react to a Pathare Prabhu daughter-in-law. She was so negative that I had not dared to take the subject further. Avantika has probed and discovered that Mother thinks we were only good friends. That has given her a weapon which she won't be chary of using if push comes to shove. That weapon will be blunted if…I know I'm asking for an impossible favour but, somehow, I feel confident you will be kind enough to…Could you come for our wedding reception? That would settle it once and for all. I mean which girl who has been in love with a man will attend his wedding to someone else? I would be eternally grateful if you came. Will you do it for the sake of our friendship? We have been the closest friends for two years, haven't we? We've shared so much, good times and bad…

With fingers crossed
Vijay

Mugdha walks straight to the bathroom and has a cold shower. She feels she has finally washed a louse called Vijay out of her hair. She comes out and tears up his letter, not savagely, just matter-of-factly. She stands on the terrace slapping the last drops of water out of her hair. Returning to her room, she takes an ordinary piece of paper and writes, 'Of course I'll come. To wish you all happiness in your marital (she scratches that out) conjugal (she scratches that out) married life. I hope to have the invitation card BY POST to know where and when I am to come.'

On December 26, 2018, she is at Vanita Samaj, Dadar with a very large present. She is wearing a Kerala sari, off white with a broad pure gold border and a deep yellow blouse. She walks into the open-air venue, past three girls who are welcoming guests with a spray of rose water, attar on the wrist and a tired looking rose. She walks straight to the end of the queue waiting to greet the couple. Vijay is in a dark suit and Avantika in a turquoise Paithani. All very traditional and classy. Mugdha looks around. She is one of the few dusky people present in a sea of light-skinned, light-eyed, supercilious looking men and women.

'Gosh, what a lucky escape,' Mugdha thinks, smiling to herself.

Walking up the red carpet that covers the rickety steps to the stage, she senses several pairs of eyes trained on her. She walks on looking directly into one pair, Vijay's.

'This is my very old and very dear friend Mugdha,' Vijay introduces her to Avantika. Avantika's smile is surprised. Mugdha's amused. Mugdha hands over her gift.

'Oh, you shouldn't have,' Vijay protests.

'How could I not? Old friends always give gifts,' she counters.

'Photo, photo,' someone calls. Mugdha stands between Avantika and Vijay's mother as two cameras click.

'You must stay for dinner,' Vijay's mother urges.

'Oh I can't,' Mugdha says smiling apologetically. 'I have two more weddings to attend.' And off she goes home on an ebullient wave of relief.

The presents are spread out on the faux marble floor of the fifteenth floor apartment in Tardeo. The house guests lounge around chewing the cud over the wedding, the officiating bhatji's nasal singing, the reception and the food. Vijay's mother looks proudly around. She has managed it all single-handed. They compliment her on her good taste and efficiency. Vijay is all smiles. Avantika wears an inscrutable expression. Vijay's mother casts questioning glances at her, unsure of how their power equation is going to work out. She decides not to worry about it just yet. Let them have their honeymoon. Plenty of time afterwards to show who rules the roost.

'I'm going to open the presents,' Vijay announces. They start with the envelopes filled with cash. They proceed to small boxes that contain cuff links and ties and silverware and twin designer watches. Then to the larger parcels with bedsheets and towels marked His and Hers. Soon they come to the elephant in the room, the very large package they both remember Mugdha giving. They undo the wrappings. Inside lies the quilt, gleaming with its silk and satin patches. Nobody has ever seen a wedding gift like that. A quilt the size of a double bed, a quilt bursting with colour.

'That is just too beautiful,' Avantika says, involuntarily.

Vijay finds his tongue. 'She spends all her time doing this kind of thing.'

Vijay's mother looks fondly at him. 'I'm telling you, she was after you. I guessed it the first day she came here.'

'What nonsense, Aai,' Vijay's voice has an edge.

'Men don't know what women know,' his mother says archly. Some of the women guests giggle.

'Why are you going to Ujjain of all places for your honeymoon?' a cousin asks.

'Because Ujjain was once called Avanti and Avantika means princess of Avanti.' Vijay glances indulgently at his bride. 'I want her to see her kingdom.'

'A kingdom without a palace. Only temples. How can you have a honeymoon surrounded by temples?'

'We aren't staying in Ujjain. We are staying in a palace in Indore. At least a hotel that has palace in its name. Five stars.'

'You don't say. What will you do in Ujjain?'

'Kalidasa. *Meghdoota*. The greatest love poem in Sanskrit literature. And if poetry doesn't impress you, then history. The Holkars. Avantika comes from the Tatya Jog family. Tatya was the maharaja's dewan when the British took over. He made sure the Holkars continued to rule the princely state. They were entitled to a 19-gun salute and all.'

'Where are they now?'

'Who?'

'The Jogs?'

'One branch is there somewhere. Not too well off. But we'll visit them.'

Avantika and Vijay fly to Ujjain. The town turns out to be dusty and woebegone. Nobody has heard of the Jogs. They hire a taxi and go to the Kalidasa Akademy. Kalidasa, the most well-known Sanskrit poet, is now a white statue sitting under a black cloud writing with a feather quill. You can't spend too much time looking at either the statue or the cloud or the quill. They get back into their cab and drive to Indore. They arrive at the Sheraton Grand Palace as night falls.

Vijay is excited. He sits on the foam bed bouncing up and down. He gives Avantika an inviting look. She notices the look but does not respond. Vijay decides there is plenty of time. He orders dinner in. Why waste time going down to the dining room? He has a shower and urges Avantika to have one too. The shower gel has an exotic scent. He wants to smell it on her. She comes out of the shower with nothing on. He is taken aback. His hope that they could disrobe together is dashed. Now it is suddenly action time. He says a little sheepishly, 'I'm a virgin.'

He assumes she is too. She says nothing. He does not notice that she guides his fumbling expertly till he has achieved what he had been waiting for. The great coming. When they go down to breakfast the next morning, his chest is proudly puffed out. Her face is inscrutable.

They stay in bed for three days and nights. He wants to experiment with all the ideas he has been storing up for this time. She is accommodating of all of them. He falls suddenly in love with her.

On their last night in Indore, he says, 'We must make a trip to the Sarafa. We can always say we saw the glass palace and the rest of the stuff. But we can't fib about the Sarafa.'

They set out. The night is bright and cold. The moon and stars glitter above the lights of the food bazaar. The streets are as crowded as they were warned at the hotel reception. They have an itinerary in hand and mean to eat their way through all its recommendations. They start with Joshiji ke dahiwade and end with Jai Bhole's jalebi and Anna's paan.

It is at the paani puri stall that they break the concentrated silence of serious eating with laughter. Avantika is having a hard time stuffing an entire loaded puri into her mouth. When Vijay stuffs the first one into his mouth, his eyes become saucers with the effort of keeping the spicy water from gushing into his throat and bringing on a coughing fit. Avantika looks comical to him. He looks comical to her. Once the puris are safely in, they laugh, their heads thrown back.

Back in Bombay they notice that their room has been arranged for them by Vijay's mother. It is a largish room, the larger of the two bedrooms in the flat, that is, not counting the half that builders offer as an option to families with a limited budget but big expectations. The calculation when Vijay's father booked the flat was simple. The parents would have one bedroom, Vijay would have the other. In time that would become his conjugal bedroom. When the two grandchildren came, first the boy, then the girl, they would have the half bedroom. Cosy with bunk beds and a cupboard for toys.

Well-made plans don't always work out. Vijay's father died within a few months of receiving the keys to the new flat. He had had one of those heart attacks that come on in the early hours of the morning and leave people saying, 'He was fine when he went to bed. He had a full dinner too. Amras-puri. He even watched news on TV before he went to bed.'

Vijay's mother had instantly gone into self-denial mode. 'What do I need a big bedroom for now? I'll sleep in the half bedroom. After all, for my remaining years, I will be only half a person.' Thereafter, the immediate and extended family's mission in life became 'Make Kamaltai happy'. They let her believe she had arranged Vijay's marriage single-handed from seeing and vetting girls to drawing up lists of relatives to whom Avantika's parents were expected to give gifts. The family elders swore Kamaltai had not looked so happy even when Vijay was born.

Avantika's mother had taken equal pleasure in planning the wedding, shopping and booking the venue and caterer. Avantika's father's only job had been to keep his cheque book open. He had smiled smugly each time he wrote out a cheque. He was pleased at having enough and more in his account to give his only child a lavish wedding and her in-laws a handsome dowry. There was no cultural friction for Avantika between her mother's and her mother-in-law's lifestyle and values. She slid into the routine of her new home like a fish into water.

'I might have wanted to arrange the room my way,' she murmurs to Vijay when they return from Indore; but it isn't a serious complaint. She will be away at the office all day and she isn't as keen a home-maker as her mother-in-law appeared to be. She doesn't seriously mind the false foliage on top of the bookshelf which holds Vijay's school and college books, fondly preserved for his children to look at. 'Baba's books? Really? Wow!'

Vijay has a more disturbing complaint than Avantika's.

'What's that quilt doing on the bed?' he demands of his mother. She instantly looks hurt.

'I thought Avantika liked it.'

'Of course I do. I think it's lovely,' Avantika responds brightly.

Vijay looks at her, hurt. They have not disagreed about anything from the time the suspicion about Mugdha had been settled and Vijay doesn't want to start now.

That night, he can't make love.

In fact, he can't make love the next night either, nor any night of the week that follows.

'You've exhausted yourself,' Avantika suggests, giggling,

Vijay is not amused. 'It's that damned quilt. She's put some witchcraft into it.'

'What nonsense, Vijay. She's your closest friend. Unless...she was in love with you. Unless...you were in love with her. Unless as people said, you were practically engaged to her.'

'You're talking rubbish.'

'Am I? You think I was taken in by that show you two put up at the reception? Would I rather not believe people who had seen you together like a couple of lovebirds?'

'Ha! As if you'd have agreed to marry me if you had really believed that.'

'Vijay dear, I agreed to marry you precisely because I believed it was true.'

Vijay's face goes totally blank.

'Let me explain,' Avantika says, crossing her legs comfortably on the quilt-covered bed. 'I am in love with Vikram Gore at the office.' She pauses to make sure Vijay has absorbed the information. He has not. She repeats, 'I am in a relationship with Vikram Gore at the office.'

All the blood drains out of Vijay's face.

'What I thought was,' Avantika continues, 'We could marry and you could continue with what's-her-name and I with Vikram. I mean I will, anyway. But I won't feel guilty if you have what's-her-name in your life.'

'But I broke off with her for your sake,' Vijay wails.

'For your mother's sake, Vijay. Let's not play games.'

'Who's this Vikram? Tell me that. Why didn't you marry him and leave me free to...'

'Marry what's-her-name?'

'Mugdha. That's her name. Why?'

'Same reason that you didn't marry Mugdha. Wrong caste.'

'Wrong caste? Gore? What's wrong with that?'

'There are Gores and Gores, Papa said. Vikram was the wrong one. Right one for me though. Look. Shall we stop fussing about this? Let's do first things first. Take that damned quilt back to Mugdha tomorrow since it is psyching you....'

Vijay bursts into tears. Avantika uncrosses her legs and runs to him in a panic.

'What are you doing? Stop it. You were brilliant in Indore.' She pats his head and holds it to her stomach. 'I know you can do it again.'

Vijay explodes. 'You think that's what's got me? My wife sits there coolly telling me she has a lover and wonders why I'm crying. I should be murdering you. Or him.'

Avantika returns to the bed and resumes her Buddha pose. She wonders if she has played this wrong. Should she have given him more time? Prepared him a little? But what the hell, what's the big deal?

'You will hand in your resignation tomorrow,' Vijay suddenly says. 'No more office for you, lady. Stay home and help Aai.'

Avantika looks at him contritely. Everyone's not made the way you are made, she tells herself. Give him time. Give him time.

'How can you sit there, tell me this…this…shameful thing and not even look ashamed.'

Avantika sighs. How much time will he need? Her patience is limited.

Vijay gets up. Strides about the room.

'Get up,' he shouts. She gets up and sits in the chair. He tears off the quilt. Throws it on the floor. 'Come here,' he commands. He tears off her nightie.

'Get into bed,' he roars.

She gets into bed. He thrusts himself into her. And comes.

Then he cries big hot tears. She holds his head to her chest.

'Now,' she says. 'Will you take that quilt away tomorrow? Talk to Mugdha. Make it up to her. For all you know she is pining for you. Give her a break.'

'She isn't pining for me. She's not like that.'

'Oh dear. Find someone else then. There must be many young things in your office waiting for a glance from you. You are more than personable you know. I'd say you are handsome.'

'Girls? You really have no shame. I'm not like that. We have morals in this family.'

Vijay sits up. 'It's decided. You will resign tomorrow. I make enough money for us. We don't need your pittance.'

'IT has the highest paid jobs in the service sector. Your mother knows how much I make. She made inquiries. I don't think she wants to lose my money.'

'You think she wants money at the cost of her only son's happiness? How dare you think that of my mother!'

Avantika shrugs. 'Talk to her. I'll take the day off tomorrow. If she agrees with you, I'll not resign. I'll return to my parents. I am an only child too. They want to see me happy.'

'You wouldn't dare.'

'I think I would. I love Vikram.'

'Love? He believes that? You married me and he believes you love him?'

'He is mature. He understands caste. One of these days his parents will find him a girl within their caste.'

'And then? You'll have to give him up.'

'No. Unless we stop loving each other.'

Vijay springs out of bed and paces about. 'Love, love, love. What is it? It's supposed to end in marriage.'

Avantika sighs. 'Look Vijay. We are going around in circles. We look at life differently. For me a marriage is what caste-believing parents do to you. They tell you love comes after marriage. It might or might not. But that's not the real purpose of marriage. The real purpose is to make babies. We are working at that. We will have two. You will see how happy everyone will be with us. They are looking at us with great expectations already. Let's not disappoint them.'

Vijay's pace has slowed down. Now he comes to a dead halt. He looks at her, totally defeated. He flops into bed, turns his back on her and goes to sleep.

❧

It is late January. The sun sets early. The terrace is already in shadow by the time Mugdha stirs from her shavaasan. For the first time since December 26, she has felt one in mind and body. The grant she had applied for has come through. She has proposed a massive study of the quilt-making traditions of India, an extension of the work her mother has already done, but with no sales attached. She will write a book with lots of photographs. A brilliant photographer has started working for the NGO, a soft-spoken man with a beard. K. Sujith. She doesn't know what K stands for. She will find out in time if she needs to. For the present, he answers to Sujith. They will make field trips to villages in Bengal, Gujarat, Karnataka and of course Maharashtra. She is excited.

She picks up her mat, rolling it up as she walks into the house. She thinks she hears the doorbell. She slides the carved cover of the eyehole up. Vijay stands outside with a large bundle in his arms. She puts her hand to her head in resignation. Will he never disappear?

She opens the door.

Vijay walks in, places the bundle on a chair and flops down in another.

'I'm famished,' he says. 'Can I persuade you to make pohe?'

Mugdha stands before him staring.

'I'll explain. I'll explain. Just give me a moment. Three flights of stairs. They always knock me out.'

Mugdha goes into the kitchen, and brings out a glass of water on a tray. She is still standing.

'Won't you sit down?'

'You mean this is a long visit?'

'Mugdha, don't be like that. Haven't you forgiven me yet?'

'I don't know. I haven't been thinking of you much.'

'And here I am thinking of you every minute of the day.'

Mugdha stares. Then looks at the bundle on the chair.

'Okay. I'll explain. That's the quilt. Avantika doesn't like it. Jealous. Yes. Our little drama didn't help. She knew too much already. Finally, I had to confess I was madly, madly in love with you.'

Vijay looks at Mugdha. 'Since you won't sit down, I'll stand up.'

Mugdha stares.

'She quarrelled every night. Take that quilt back, she kept saying. Wouldn't talk to me. Aai got suspicious. I couldn't bear for Aai to be unhappy.'

'Of course you couldn't.'

Vijay's shoulders droop in relief.

'You see that, don't you?'

'I've always seen that.'

'She can't. She won't. Finally, I agreed to bring the quilt back. Not unhappily. It was a chance to see you again.'

'Right. Would you like to go now?'

'Come on, Mugdha. Can't we be friends? I want to come and see you...'

Mugdha has walked to the door and is holding it open.

Standing before her, he says, 'I've never loved anyone as I have loved you, Mugdha. Perhaps you need more time. I was stupid to think you would forgive me so soon. I'll come again. In another month? Two. I can't keep away forever darling. I love you.' He grabs her hand. It is cold. She pulls it away.

'You might find this very, very hard to believe, Vijay, but I don't love you. I often wonder how I ever did. You are totally and utterly pathetic. Now go.'

Mugdha shuts the door as soon as he steps out. Vijay stands outside sobbing. She can hear him through the door. In the very moment that she hears him sobbing, she knows he wants her to hear him. She leans against the door, her heart heavy for Vijay.

Ears Apart

A storyteller must be upfront with the reader if she knows she has a particular leaning towards or away from a character she has created. That's my principle. If you are about to say that any such leanings should reveal themselves in the telling of the story, then you have more faith in the reader than I do. I have had a chap come up to me and say, 'I didn't mind you making fun of me in your last story but it hurt my mother deeply. And she is nearing ninety.' I did not know him from Valmiki, but he had seen himself in my story, in a character with whom (not at whom) I had been indulgently, fondly laughing. Although a fiction writer should love all her characters equally, this fiction writer's heart just happens not to be big enough for that. I will therefore confess that, in the case of this story, I do not care much for Chandrakant, the protagonist. I would therefore urge all Chandrakants out there to keep the story away from their mothers, especially if they are nearing ninety.

I need to make another confession. A storyteller who expects her readers to take her story seriously must make sure she fills it with every realistic detail that she can think up to flesh out her characters and their locations. I will confess I have fallen short on this count earlier and been roundly chastised by readers for short-changing them. Fact is, I am not interested in personal detail. Some details, particularly in my society where offence is taken with every sip of tea, become tricky. For instance, Chandrakant has no surname. Rather, he has a surname but I have chosen to keep it to myself because a surname is an instant indicator of caste and caste is trouble for someone who has already declared that she does not like the character. In no time readers in Vile Parle and Girgaon and Chinchpokali will infer that this (w)itch of a so-called story-writer who does not like one of us, actually does not like any of us because, in fact, she is against our caste as a whole. Therefore, Chandrakant goes without a surname. Other than that, I have tried to flesh him out with as much detail as I could create.

Having prefaced a slight story with a substantial disclaimer, I shall now proceed to narrate it.

Chandrakant is forty years old on this day, 21 December 1998. He will remain forty during the real-time narration of the story and for the rest of the day till midnight. Come one minute past midnight, he will step into his forty-first year.

Chandrakant's hair has turned to salt above the ears. And yet, simple man that he is, he still visits the same barber, Kool Kut Kesh Kartanalaya, whom he discovered in his last year at school and whom he has asked for the same haircut for the quarter of a century that has elapsed since.

Chandrakant's complexion is the colour of a certain strain of wheat called Khandwa that makes soft chapattis when mixed half-and-half with another strain called Punjab Pishi, but by itself leans towards leather. His height is as exact a 165 cm as you can get. He takes 16-inch collar shirts. His shoulders slope approximately 45 degrees from the horizontal. His girth around the middle is 25 cm more than his girth around the chest. That puts a strain on the fifth button of his shirt when he is seated. The last Sunday of every month, after tea and pohe, his wife Shalini pulls out her sewing kit and, while engaged in small talk about family matters with Chandrakant, she tightens the fifth buttons on all his laundered shirts stacked on the intricately carved stool next to her. Chandrakant watches her with tender admiration as she bites off the cotton between her small, even, pearl-white teeth with every button done.

The colour of Chandrakant's tailor-made shirts, whether checked or lined, hovers around cream with blue, cream with grey or cream with coffee. His trousers, of the best available fabric and well cut, tend towards slate grey. Ten years ago, Shalini had, just for the heck of it, as a joke really, had the tailor make him a bright red shirt. She had presented it to him, giggling, the day before they were leaving for a birthday break in Mahabaleshwar. He had worn it too on the celebratory day. 'How handsome you look,' she had said more than once. Chandrakant had blushed. The hotel had arranged for a cake and had lined up their photographer to take a picture of Chandrakant cutting it. That photograph, framed, stands in their living room as concrete evidence of Chandrakant having once worn a red shirt. Shalini had known he would never wear it in Mumbai. Nor did he, having curated his image of a responsible finance manager-to-be even when he was an apprentice in his first job.

Chandrakant believes he is most fortunate to have as intelligent and devoted a wife as Shalini. Despite having a Master's degree in psychology, she has led a happy life as cook, cleaner, breeder and rearer. If he has climbed the professional ladder as steadily as he has, it is entirely because she has shouldered all family responsibilities including, most importantly, bringing up their sons Rajeev and Sachin as responsible young men with bright careers ahead.

Shalini considers herself equally fortunate in having as intelligent and appreciative a husband as Chandrakant, a rare male specimen who, unbelievably, has no addictions. Forget smoking and drinking (we will not even mention womanising), he has not been known to put a single sliver of betelnut or a shred of paan in his mouth. The family vouches one hundred per cent for this.

At the time of the present events, Chandrakant stands comfortably a little way below the topmost rung of GoliMar & Sons Finance Corp. As a realist, he knows there is little chance of his being appointed to the top job. That is reserved for '& Sons'. But he has every hope of making it to the head honcho's right hand. He has allowed his dreams to run with certitude towards that desired end.

Earlier this year, on the auspicious occasion of Vijaya Dashami, he handed over the keys to his white Maruti 800 to Shalini and himself took charge of the keys to a brand new burgundy coloured Esteem. Of course, he has the use of the office car with chauffeur. But he likes driving his Esteem to the office, particularly because it allows him to enjoy another bit of luxury—listening to his CDs of Ghulam Ali's ghazals on the car's audio system. His love of ghazals, a mark of refined sentiment, finds an emotional response in Shalini. They are as perfectly attuned to each other in matters of cultural sensibility as they are in matters of moral values. When Chandrakant says spontaneously, as he occasionally might, 'Shalini look, the moon is gleaming like a silver coin' or 'Ah the heady fragrance of rain-soaked earth' or 'Where has this rippling breeze come from? Where could it be going?' Shalini shakes her head in wonderment and looks at him with moist eyes.

On this day, 21 December 1998, there is a distinct nip in the air. Chandrakant turns off the air-conditioning, rolls down the windows and lets the cool fresh air play in his greying hair. He loves nature. He occasionally drives with rolled down windows in the monsoons, to let in the raindrops, feeling adventurous and pleased to be one with nature.

As Chandrakant drives down Dr Annie Besant Road at an easy speed, the cool air playing about his face, he listens to Ghulam Ali singing *Chupke chupke raat din ansoo bahana yaad hai* in an intimate voice, as though he is telling Chandrakant alone that he remembers shedding tears secretly day and night. Such delicious melancholy. As the ghazal proceeds, Chandrakant's heart suffers the familiar twinge that comes with the awakening of an old, old memory. His love for Shalini has never caused him such pain. Perhaps pain is the companion of unrequited love? Of course it is. Why would you feel pain for something you have?

As he allows his disciplined heart to wallow a little in pain, it slips out of his control and misses a beat. Simultaneously, he shifts in his seat. Simultaneously, his palms burst into sweat. Simultaneously his scalp itches. The reason for these unusual manifestations stands at the bus-stop which he has just passed. He slows down to take another look in the rearview mirror. The disturbing reason at the bus-stop is slim, clad in a green sari topped by a patterned choli. Her outsize glares notwithstanding, he knows at once it is she. He breaks into a fresh sweat. His burgundy Esteem comes to an unbidden stop and parks itself by the kerb. His eyes are fixed on the rear-view mirror. His suspicion is confirmed. 'It is she. Bharati,' he mutters to Ghulam Ali.

The fact established, he plans to restart the car and continue his interrupted journey. But his hands refuse to do his bidding. When the car moves, it is in reverse gear. Chandrakant is compelled to decide the car is right. He really ought to offer Bharati a lift. How terrible to see her stand at a bus-stop like a waif. She deserves better. But how will he look offering her a lift? Like a lech attempting an easy pick-up? He has recognised her. But is it not an unwarranted leap of the ego to imagine she will recognise him after so many... twenty-five years?

Chandrakant takes a quick decision with the efficiency that comes naturally to men in his position. He tears a page out of the notebook in which he secretly writes his own ghazals and scribbles, 'Bharati, this is Chandrakant from Holiday Home Khandala twenty-five years ago. We sat on the water tank after dinner every day chatting into the night. I would like to offer you a lift. You will find my burgundy-coloured Esteem parked about 100 ft up from the bus-stop.' Chandrakant beckons a little urchin who is ambling down the road with bunches of flowers, presses a crisp ten-rupee note in his grubby palm and points to the madam at the bus-stop. He watches Bharati as she reads the note, looks in his direction, glances in the other direction to see if her bus is coming. Then begins to walk slowly towards the car. He reverses, his heart pounding, to meet her halfway. He opens the door. She slides in beside him and says, 'Hullo!'

'You recognised me,' he says as he starts the car.

'Actually no,' she says running her eyes frankly over his face.

'But you accepted my lift...'

'I remember Khandala and the tank. So you couldn't be some common or garden lech.'

'Ah you do remember Khandala then.' Chandrakant's armpits stop pricking.

'Of course I do,' she grins, her eyes taking on a special shine as she says the words. Aha! thinks Chandrakant. She hasn't recognised me yet. But she will when I remind her of that night!

They were sitting on the tank as usual. The stars glittered above. The cool air of the Sahyadris brought memories of Hindi films. They sang songs of romance, love, separation. Then there was silence. Suresh said, 'I'll tell you a ghost story. A true story. It really happened.' Chandrakant was sitting next to Bharati. Shekhar in front of them, practically in his lap. Behind him sat Ujjwala and Gargi. Ashok and Ravi were somewhere around. The story began. As it progressed, the two girls at the back pressed against him. At one point, Suresh's hero entered the haunted house. A door creaked open. Two icy hands wound themselves around his neck. The girls behind him screamed. Chandrakant felt concerned for Bharati. He reached out for her hand. She kept it tightly gripped in his till the end of the story.

'You remember the night of the ghost story, don't you?' Chandrakant smiles.

'Don't I just.' Her eyes shine even more brightly now.

'Then you must remember who was sitting next to you."

'Oh the usual lot.'

'But specifically, who?'

'Shekhar.'

'You remember him? And Chandrakant?'

'Not the faintest.'

Chandrakant swallows and brings out, with great difficulty, "Reedy Weedy? You remember Reedy Weedy?'

Bharati turns swiftly in her seat. She gazes at Chandrakant's face with fresh interest and bursts into a gale of laughter.

'Of course. That's what Shekhar used to call you. You were too. Skinny as a reed. What a relief. It's all coming back now.' She slaps him on the back.

Chandrakant's throat has gone dry. He drives solemnly, his eyes on the road ahead, not allowing his turbulent thoughts to interfere with his concentration, thereby keeping the old and the young, the able and the infirm crossing the road at Kemp's corner out of harm's way. Bharati is still looking at him with the same renewed interest. A thought lights up her eyes. 'Chandya, you could wiggle your ears back then, couldn't you?'

Chandrakant is willing to face any humiliation now that she remembers the night of the ghost story, the night she allowed him to hold her trembling hand and give her courage. His flag is flying high. Nothing will bring it down.

'After Khandala, I tried hard for days to wiggle mine. But you think I could?'

'You couldn't?'

'Of course I couldn't. I have dunce ears. Nothing moves them.' Bharati inspects Chandrakant's ears with close attention. 'There's no difference in the structure as far as I can see. Why can you wiggle yours and I can't mine?'

Chandrakant manages to muster a smile. 'Ears apart…' he begins

'Can you still do it?'

'No.' Chandrakant's voice is firm. 'There's no time in my busy schedule for such things.'

'Come on. I'm not asking if you wiggle them every day like you shave every day. Once in a while. Just for fun. To amuse your children. You have children, don't you? Hasn't Papa shown them his magic trick ever?'

'No.' Chandrakant senses a lump in his throat like those marbles that stoppered old aerated drink bottles.

'Then you must show me.'

'What nonsense.'

'Why not?'

'Out of the question.'

'Come on Chandya. Don't be such a stuck up. You'd do it at the drop of a hat in Khandala.'

Chandrakant's shoulders fall. His face goes rigid. His eyes scan the road to see if anyone is watching. Then, very quickly, he wiggles both ears. Up-down, up-down, up-down and done. Bharati bursts into peals of laughter. Chandrakant joins in weakly. A hollow laugh.

Bharati says in between laughing, 'You have to do this for your kids. Really. Anybody can buy an Esteem. How many can wiggle their ears?'

They are approaching Bharatiya Vidya Bhavan where she wants to be dropped. 'Thank God I remembered you. It would have bothered me all day if I hadn't.'

'What about the ghost story? You said you remembered that.'

'I do, I do.'

'Remember how scared you were?'

'Me? Good heavens no. The girls behind me were. And the chap next to me. When the ghost wound his icy hands around the hero's neck, this fellow gripped my hand and wouldn't let go. I had to hold it tight it was trembling so hard. Clammy as a toad's back I tell you.'

When Bharati alights from the car at Vidya Bhavan, she pokes her head back in through the window. 'Thank you. Really. For recognising me after all these years, giving me a lift and…and wiggling your ears.' She laughs again, withdraws her head and dances away.

❧

If truth be told, the story has ended. I should thank my Muse for having supplied me with a good exit line for Bharati. But how can I leave a character for whom I have already confessed a lack of whole-hearted sympathy, high and dry during his most vulnerable moments? I have made a public display of the deflation of his high-flying balloon. I consider it my duty to give an account of how he will repair the puncture and ensure that the balloon returns to its erstwhile height.

The very moment that Bharati turns her back on Chandrakant to walk breezily away, he starts his Esteem, revs her up and speeds away. He maintains, all the way down Marine Drive, the demeanour of one who has suffered no affront to his dignity. It is not an easy thing to do. Draupadi laughed and the great Kurukshetra war happened. If Bharati's laughter causes him to grind the accelerator into the car floor, one would understand. But his foot is merely firm, not reckless, while he makes the following therapeutic remarks to himself with dramatic pauses in between.

I didn't spot a mangalsutra around her neck.

She doesn't look so good now.

Youth makes everyone look good. Real beauty defies time.

Wonder why she hasn't married.

Takes two to marry.

Who knows. She might even be a feminist.

She's obviously not well-off. Travels by bus.

The way she used to ogle Shekhar in those days…

Say what you will, modesty is a woman's true ornament.

By the time Chandrakant reaches Nariman Point, his shoulders are back to 45 degrees from the horizontal. His blood has resumed its smooth flow through his veins. His face is aglow with quiet self-confidence. Walking to his cabin he acknowledges his secretary's respectful 'good morning, sir' graciously. Leaning back in his executive chair, he looks at the polished surface of his expansive desk, free as always of papers, they having been disposed of efficiently by the end of the previous day, and decides to call Shalini. His wife's concerned hello warms his heart. 'Is anything the matter?' she asks, her voice tinged with worry.

'Nothing at all…or perhaps a lot.'

'Is this a time for riddles with my morning chores waiting to be done?' she asks in mock displeasure.

'Love, love is the biggest riddle. I drove to work with the cool winter breeze on my face, Ghulam Ali's

Chupke chupke raat din in my ears and warm thoughts of you in my heart. I decided to call. Is that wrong? You're my wife, after all.'

Shalini, at her end, breaks out in goosebumps. Chandrakant, at his, sighs happily into the phone and gets down to work.

She Came to Stay

Her name is Savitri, and she is not a pativrata. In fact, her aesthetics reject the form in which pativratas are portrayed—bent head, cow eyes, hands folded. Chhat! Why? An erect woman with squared shoulders can love, can't she? But who wants love when devotion is on offer?

Etc etc.

Those are the kind of thoughts Savitri amuses herself with as she throws elegant pots and mugs and vases in her studio. Right now, as she marches down Nepean Sea Road, her thoughts are anything but amusing. She has left behind, in the shadowy interiors of Sizzling Platter, her husband feeding a woman in red, a delicate spoonful of tiramisu. That was the last straw for her already frazzled nerves. She crumpled her napkin, flung it down beside her half-eaten lava cake, pushed her chair back, stood up and said loud and clear, 'You're welcome to feed each other for the rest of your lives. I'm quitting.'

The other diners allowed themselves a barely raised eyebrow before returning to their artichoke hearts. Savitri's husband too, pretending nothing had happened, continued to coax the woman in red to try a nibble of tiramisu from his spoon. But the woman was in shock. She stared fixedly at the table cloth, muttering, 'This is very awkward. You said she'd be cool with us.'

'As she should have been,' Savitri's husband said shaking his head. 'Don't know what got into her. Probably menopausing.'

'At her age? Don't be ridiculous.'

'She started her periods at ten. Maybe twenty-five years is enough?'

'You're impossible. I had said no PDA.'

'Feeding you tiramisu is PDA? Why are you so scared? Your husband's in his study in Delhi writing a book.'

'I think we are through. Please call for the bill.'

She insisted on paying. He did not demur. They left. She slipped into her car; he decided to visit his brother.

But Savitri's husband and the woman in red are not our protagonists. Savitri is. She is, even now, striding down Nepean Sea Road looking straight ahead and feeling a little abashed at her behaviour. It is a long walk home and she needs it to clear her head. If the walk doesn't help, she means to drop in on Ram. He plays the flute and has a profoundly calming influence on her.

It is late. Shop shutters are coming down. Vegetable

and fruit stalls are being covered with blue tarpaulin sheets secured firmly with coir rope. Savitri lives on the twentieth floor and Ram on the fifteenth of a high-rise at the end of the road. I am not one to miss out on concrete detail, like names of buildings; but I cannot for the life of me remember what this one is called. Perhaps because the name is ridiculously grandiloquent and sadly in keeping with the mish-mash architecture of the building itself.

We will leave Savitri walking the last few hundred metres to her destination, while I do a quick sketch of her. She is petite, wears her hair in a bouncy bob, is a potter who holds an annual sold-out show at a boutique gallery in an old mill compound in Parel, now upgraded to chic gentility. She is childless by choice, bohemian in lifestyle and tends to let her mind wander in the middle of conversations. We have already met Savitri's husband whose name, by the way, is Narendra.

Ram, Savitri's anchor, is a Tata man, proud to be so. He has an eighteen-year-old daughter, a stable body and an equable temperament. Ram's wife lives somewhere in the 15th Arondissement, Paris, having run off with a Frenchman five years into their marriage, leaving Ram literally holding the baby whom they had fondly named Anisha, constant light.

Savitri enters her high-rise and takes the elevator to the twentieth floor. Her mental state is still far from stable. She packs a bag, descends to the fifteenth floor and stands outside Ram's door. She hears Ram playing a meditative Megh alap on his flute, in consonance with the clouds that have gathered to cover the face of the moon. Thundershowers have been predicted. The weekend will be flooded. She wonders if she should ring the doorbell. She does not want to stop the music. She rings.

Ram opens the door. He is dressed in his home clothes, lungi and sadra, which Savitri considers cute for a Tata man. He waves the hand holding the flute to welcome her in. But his face looks apprehensive and his heart pounds. It is 11 p.m. on a Friday night, minutes away from his bedtime. But that is not reason enough for the nervous face and the pounding heart. To explain that, I must digress.

Last year, that is in 2010, in June to be precise, on the twentieth of the month to be even more precise, when Anisha was visiting her mother in Paris, Ram had fallen in a faint at home. Saraswatibai, his devoted cook-cum-housekeeper-cum-baby-sitter, had rushed to fetch Dr Punwani from the seventeenth floor, then rushed to the twentieth floor to inform Savitribai and Narendrasaheb. The doctor had rushed to the fifteenth floor, examined Ram and pronounced him fit but in dire need of rest.

'Tatas don't run on you alone,' he had scolded. 'You're married to the damned company.'

Dr Punwani had then turned to Savitri. 'Please make

sure he stays at home, mostly in bed if possible, for at least a week.'

Narendra was leaving on a trek for the travel book he was writing; but Savitri would be more than happy to keep an eye on Ram she said. Ram said nothing, sure that he could slip out to work for a few hours and slip back in before Savitri got home from her studio. Saraswatibai had no idea what Dr Punwani had said. He would tell her the fainting fit was caused by a touch of low blood pressure which the doctor had set right with a tablet.

But Savitri had other ideas. She had walked into his home that night with a bag stuffed to bursting with lounging clothes.

'Decided to move in,' she had announced cheerfully. 'Can't trust you corporate types. You'd have slipped out to work and back again before I came home from the studio. That's not going to happen. I've taken a week off my pots and mugs. I'm going to make sure you follow Hiru's orders to a tee.'

The week that followed had been the most exciting of his dietary life. Ever since Anisha had started college, she had eaten less and less at home. She was always 'hanging out' with her gang. Saraswatibai would scold him, 'You are her father. She's learning books. But she's still a girl. It's not good for her to be out day and night.'

Ram would reply, 'You have a right over her too. You helped me bring her up. Why don't you tell her? I don't know how.'

Saraswatibai had tried. And failed. And Ram had settled into a daily routine of roti-bhaji-dal which left Saraswatibai feeling immensely depressed. The only change she was allowed to make to the routine was jowar bhakri and baigan bharta on Sundays.

With Savitri installed in the house fired by the mission of looking after Ram in every which way, meaning culinarily too, the week's repertoire turned international—moussaka, Thai curry, penne and eggplant gratin, stuffed cabbage leaves, crepes, borshch which way back in 1998 the *New York Times* had declared 'humble no more' and, returning to her roots, sai bhaji. Saraswatibai rose to the occasion, helping Savitri cut and chop, fry and steam. She even ate these things that she had never seen or tasted before. Savitri took a picture of her tearing crepes with her fingers and dipping them in dal.

At night, when Saraswatibai left, Ram played the flute and Savitri sipped Cointreau. On the last day of the week, she had walked over from her easy chair to the settee where Ram was playing *Ras ke bhare tore nain,* Radha's plaint to the Dark One that she would find no rest till she had seen his love-filled eyes. Savitri had lowered herself noiselessly onto the settee and laid her head on Ram's shoulder. His fingers had frozen mid-note. 'Please play on,' she had urged softly. 'Be with the music. Not me.'

When the music ended, she had stood up, stretched

out her hand and led Ram to her room where they made love. He did not know how it had happened. He wasn't sure that it had happened at all. But it had. He should not have done it. He really should not have.

Ram had taken a few months after that week to return to equilibrium. And now Savitri is in the house again bearing a bag bursting with clothes.

'I've left Narendra,' she announces, walking to the bar to pour herself a tot of brandy. Her back is to him so he has time to readjust his face and posture.

'So where are you off to?' he asks with no real curiosity, because he knows the answer.

She turns around and says, predictably, 'Here.'

'Anisha is not in Paris,' he says evenly. 'She is here.'

Savitri looks at Ram's face and bursts out laughing. 'I'll sleep out here on the settee.'

'Rubbish,' Ram responds feeling his entire body, including his heart, relax. 'I will sleep here. You can have the bed.'

'Impossible. It's a double bed. King size. I'll sleep in it only if you share it with me.'

Seeing Ram's face Savitri lets out another peel of laughter. 'Really Ram, women are not equipped to rape. If you like, we can put a bolster between us in case I stray in the middle of the night.' He declines the offer. She insists on the alternative. The settee. Just then Anisha walks in and gives Savitri a hug.

'How do you feel about your father and I sleeping in

the same bed?' Savitri could be asking Anisha whether she wanted tea or coffee.

Ram goes red in the face and shakes his head vigorously but Savitri isn't looking at him.

'I don't think Papa will sleep a wink,' Anisha says seriously. 'Look at him. He's jelly already.'

Both women laugh. 'But tell you what,' Anisha says, still giggling. 'You can have my bed and I'll sleep on the settee. Only, I'll have to use the bathroom. How long is it for?'

'All my life,' Sita says grimly.

'Right. Over the weekend then.' Anisha goes into her room and brings out an armful of stuff. Then her earphones go on and she's lost to the world. Savitri sits in the easy chair sipping brandy. Ram is on the settee with his flute.

'Play for me,' Savitri says moving to the settee. Ram gets up casually and moves to the easy chair.

'Something soulful,' Savitri says. 'A quiet Bhairavi.'

Ram begins to play and within five minutes Savitri is snoring lightly.

'I'll make up the bed. You carry her in,' Anisha says.

'Me?'

'Since I can't. She's lightweight, Papa. What's the matter with you?'

Ram carries Savitri to Anisha's bed. Once she is in, he cannot but pull a sheet over her and tuck her in. Once he has tucked her in, he cannot but linger for a few moments looking down at her face.

The cantankerous reunion between Savitri and Narendra happens on Sunday night just after Saraswatibai has left. They have finished dinner and stacked the used plates in the sink for her to attack the following morning, when the doorbell rings.

Ram opens the door. Narendra strolls in and throws himself into the easy chair. 'Phew! What an evening,' he says.

There's a long pause. 'At Bhai's place,' he explains. 'They fought. They don't have much to do with both boys away. So they fight. Usha screeches. Bhai roars. I sneaked out. I could hear them halfway down the road.' Narendra glances at Savitri. 'And what came over you suddenly back then? I've never seen you look so livid.'

'Maybe because I have never been so livid!'

'So why? What? I said to her you must be menopausing.'

'You did, did you? And what did she say?'

'You're too young for that.'

'That I am. And she's too old to be fed. I hope she liked the tiramisu.'

'What tiramisu? The woman is crazy. After you left, she kept looking around like a scared rabbit as though her husband was going to pop out of somebody's hat. She has been totally fascinating otherwise. She's researching musical instruments of the north-east—how they are made, who makes them, how long they've been made in the same way, how they are played, the lot. She'll either write a book or make a documentary film. She's terrific in private. But in public she was impossible. She refused to stay after you left. She looked like a woman of the world didn't she, Savu? But hardcore Maniben under that seductive red thing she was wearing.'

'So, no second act?'

'You know there wasn't. You must have noticed we weren't at breakfast.'

'I didn't.'

'What do you mean?'

'You didn't notice? I wasn't there.'

'How could I notice? I was at Bhai's.'

'Well then, here it is. I wasn't at breakfast because I was down here. I was down here because I've left you.'

'Left me? How could you have left me when I wasn't there to be left? Ha ha. How's that for a curveball eh Ram?'

'There's some work I need to do,' Ram muttered. 'You two carry on.' Ram got up.

'Forget work, yaar. It's Sunday night. Sit. Play us something.'

Ram's jaw drops. Savitri laughs out loud. 'Ram can't believe you want to hear music when you're facing mine. Please notice that I am very upset and I want to have it out.'

'No, Savu. Not now. Can't we do it tomorrow? Oh okay. Sit yaar Ram. I need a witness for this. I don't want her digging up the wrong mud later.' Narendra turns full face to Savitri. 'Shoot.'

'I'm pregnant.'

'Is that all?'

'And I'm not going to drop it this time.'

'What? That's totally against the letter and spirit of our marriage vows. You know that.'

At this point two things happen. Anisha walks in and Savitri lets out a long, sustained, full-throated scream. Anisha sits down in shock, Narendra looks terrified and Ram moves to Savitri, squeezes her hand and says, 'Hush.'

Savitri hushes. After that her voice comes edged with icicles of great sharpness and clarity. She makes a brief speech about the four ashramas of human life which were once confined to men only but now apply equally to women because modern women are men with breasts and wombs and she thinks it is time for her to end her bachelorhood and settle down to being a householder. If he wants to remain a young blade screwing every skirt that floats by, he is free to fuck off.

Having delivered this little speech, Savitri feels a wave of profound peace wash over her. She lowers herself into the settee, crosses her legs and smiles benignly at Narendra.

Narendra looks closely at her, shakes his head in bewilderment and says he will need time to consider the impossible options she has offered him—to fuck off or stay back and endure being a father.

'Better be snappy about it,' Savitri says. 'The second

option isn't going to be available for ever.' Then she adds, grinning, 'Conditions apply.'

Anisha, who has been observing this sample of adult behaviour pop-eyed, rises, still a little stunned, and says, 'I'll say good night guys.' Then, a little ashamed at allowing three adults to shock her, she adds, 'If you are staying on, Savitri, I guess you'll continue to share Papa's bed,' and does not stay to watch their faces.

Back on the twentieth floor, Narendra forgets the whole business of options. By the time Savitri has completed five months, she is at the end of her tether. She takes to pushing them at him every morning at breakfast. Reluctantly, he begins to weigh them. Fuck off or be a father. You call those options? He has no ongoing relationship which can be transformed into a live-in arrangement. He has a 1BHK flat in Bandra bazaar, his share from his father's property. But that is the asset he lives off. It gives him his daily bread and eggs. He cannot move in there. The third alternative is moving in with Bhai whose sons are in the US. But that means dealing with Usha whose way of dealing with Narendra whose sight she cannot endure, is to screech more than ever at Bhai. Settle down to being a father? He considers the idea distantly before dropping it quickly. It is possible he could get away with not being hands-on, but he would still have to bear baby smells. Really, Savu shouldn't have done this to him.

By the time Savitri is seven months gone, Narendra

has decided Bhai will have to deal with Usha as best he can. Narendra will take care not to be home except to sleep and wash. Meanwhile an interesting possibility has opened up in Delhi—a fellow-trekker who lost her husband to the Himalayas a few years ago, could be looking for a replacement. Her greatest asset is being the only child of a hotel chain owner. This means she has an independent bungalow to herself with enough space to allow them to live their own lives and still be together. And who knows, once the coming baby is five years old and has started school and has stopped peeing and pooping in its pants, he might want to return to Savitri and teach the child Sanskrit and astronomy. Narendra leaves for Bhai's.

Savitri is working hard towards her show. Anisha has been offered a seat at Stanford with assistance and is excitedly getting ready to go. Ram has taken leave to go with her. The only thing that is stable between floors 15 and 20 of the unnameable tower, is Saraswatibai. Every day she warns Anisha, 'Don't you dare marry a white man. We have lots of good fellows here.'

The day Anisha leaves, Saraswatibai can't stop crying into the sweepings, into the clothes, into the dough and into her pallu. Savitri strokes her back which makes her sob louder, throw her thin arms around Savitri's neck and blubber into it, 'Twenty years I have looked after her, poor motherless child. I in the day, Saheb in the evening through illness and health. Such a father I have never seen. And now she's leaving.' She detaches herself from Savitri's neck, wipes her eyes on her sari and brightens. 'But we've got another one coming. You must stay here for the first three months at least. They are a real handful then. Who'll help you up there?'

Narendra and Bhai come to the opening of the show carrying a vastly exaggerated bouquet of roses. Bhai looks appreciatively at Savitri's distended belly under her smart smock and then, even more appreciatively at his darling younger brother and says, 'Someone will soon be calling you Papa.' With what admirable ease he elides the improbability of the caller ever meeting the called for the calling to happen. The brothers leave soon after they have walked around nodding, Bhai's hand on Narendra's shoulder.

Ram has watched the drama from a far corner of the gallery, as upset as he is capable of being with Narendra. As the evening proceeds, he cannot stop asking himself what kind of a man Narendra is that he isn't excited by the idea of becoming a father?

The invitees begin to leave. Soon the gallery is empty except for the cleaning staff who get busy clearing up. Savitri sinks into a chair sighing. A minute later, she lumbers up again moaning, 'No. Oh no.' Her water has burst. She has only just completed seven months and her water has burst. Ram takes charge. He calls the hospital, rushes home to pack a few things for Savitri's hospital stay, drives her down and walks the hospital corridor all night, worrying. The baby arrives at break of day, a trifle red, a trifle wrinkled, but perfectly formed. When Saraswatibai sets eyes on her, she is wonderstruck at her brightness. 'Chandrasarkha chehra ahe ga bai,' she coos. The baby is instantly named Chandani, Chanda for short.

During Savitri's days in the hospital, Ram rushes from the gallery in Parel to the mum-and-baby shop on Nepean Sea Road every evening, till he has managed to put together a full nursery in Anisha's room—a crib, mattress, little pillow, hanging mobile, soft toys and a small wardrobe complete with swaddle wraps, quilt, towels and vests.

'Both shows successful,' Ram beams at the end of the week. 'The pots are all gone and Chanda has arrived.'

The story which began rather unpredictably perhaps, ends exactly as you are expecting it to. Ram cannot bear to be parted from Chandani and asks Savitri to marry him. Savitri says that would make her a bigamist and it's too much trouble divorcing Narendra, so she'd rather live in sin with Ram just as Narendra is doing with the hotel heiress in Delhi and Ram's wife is doing with her Frenchman in Paris. Ram's Vidarbha blood revolts against the idea for a brief moment, but he tells it to shut up because marrying Savitri would make him a bigamist too. Sobering down, he begins to move Savitri's and Chandani's things from Anisha's bedroom to his.

'You must get plenty of rest,' he says soothingly to Savitri. 'I will do night duty.'

'But the breasts are with me,' Savitri points out.

'Chanda will be brought to them when she needs them,' he assures her, holding the baby close to his chest.

For years thereafter, when Savitri gets back from the studio, Ram is already home playing quiet little tunes on his flute to a happy Chandani while his tea gets cold much to Saraswatibai's annoyance.

'May I hold my baby for a while?' Savitri asks and is granted permission with remarkable grace. While she holds the baby, Ram kneels down beside her to take the three thousandth selfie to send to Anisha. Sitting in Stanford, Anisha receives the picture with the same resignation with which she has received the previous two thousand nine hundred and ninety-nine. Once again, dutifully, she does what she is expected to do. She sends a WhatsApp message back saying 'Isn't she lovely! Absolutely gorgeous.' She adds dancing stars and pumping hearts to enhance the effect of the words. Sitting in Mumbai, Ram beams and Savitri shakes her head.

Lost Daughter

15 April 2020, 5 a.m. Anagha has drawn her final breath. For the last two hours it has been coming and going with a deep rasping sound. Now there is no breath. There is silence. Vishnu, sitting beside his daughter, has felt the hardly perceptible throb of her pulse under his fingers grow steadily weaker till this moment of sudden stilling. He lifts his eyes to Supriya sitting on the other side of the bed. She goes ashen.

It was two hours ago that they had heard something fall and roll in Anagha's room. Neither Vishnu nor Supriya had been able to sleep that night. They were out of bed and into her room in a trice, switching on lights. She must have lunged for her inhaler when the attack came. She must have been frantic. The inhaler must have slipped from her shaking fingers. She lay on her side, her arms dangling over the edge of the bed, her eyes staring. Vishnu turned her over on her back and began to look for her inhaler.

'No point looking for it,' Supriya's voice was emotionless. Anagha's lips had gone blue. Her head rolled from side to side. Her chest heaved. 'She needs a hospital.'

Vishnu called Dr Gupte. Mrs Gupte answered. 'I have not seen my husband for the last many weeks. You'll find him in the COVID ward of the hospital.'

Vishnu called the 24-hour chemist for some SOS medication. The chemist, exempt from the lockdown, was open; but the errand boy had not turned up so they could not send the medication.

Vishnu ran down and out in his night clothes. Two policemen stopped him. 'You cannot go out, Mister.'

'It's an emergency. My daughter is dying.'

'Many daughters are dying, sir. But rules are rules. Kindly go back or we'll have to arrest you, sir.'

Vishnu side-stepped them and ran for it. They chased him and caught him.

'We will not arrest you, sir. You look like an educated gentleman. We are taking you home.'

They stood guard as he climbed the stairs, shoulders down, heart splitting, spirit defeated. He could have shown the police his press card. But he had been too rushed to think of carrying it. He ran into Anagha's bedroom and sat down beside her, his fingers on her wrist, urging her pulse to hold out. But it could not. Did not. And now it is still.

Vishnu lowers his eyes from Supriya's ashen face and takes his fingers off Anagha's wrist. Caesar lifts his head and howls. Supriya sinks to the floor, holds his floppy-eared head to her chest and sobs. The slow, painful minutes of the last two hours, the peaceful face of his daughter, never immobile once she had begun to walk and talk and now silent forever, gather into a heaving surge in Vishnu's stomach. 'NO!' The word explodes from him, rushes out into the sepulchral silence of the city and dies away. There are no echoes. Just soundlessness.

They had called their daughter Anagha—the sinless, the pure, the virtuous. She should have lived to a ripe old age, loving and being loved. But here she lies at twenty-seven, lifeless. Who decides these things? Why, when he is healthy, his wife is healthy, should their daughter have asthma? From where did the condition come? Who gave her death?

'No,' Vishnu says again, but this time in a whimper.

Vishnu and Supriya cannot bear the thought of actually uttering the words to convey the news to friends and relatives. They put the words out on their WhatsApp groups, fingers trembling. 'Anagha is no more. Severe asthmatic attack.'

'You're sure it wasn't Covid? That causes breathlessness too.' One response.

'It wasn't. She was asthmatic. This was a stress-related flare-up.'

When the first photographs of migrants walking home had hit television screens and the front pages of newspapers, Anagha had paced the floor ceaselessly.

'I can't sit here under this fan while they are walking in the sun. I must walk with them,' she had said. 'I must share their pain.'

'Walk to where?' Supriya had asked impatiently. 'They are going to walk thousands of kilometres to Rajasthan and Bihar and Uttar Pradesh. Is that where you want to go?' Supriya had sighed. 'They have pain. We have comfort. That's how it is. Now stop pacing about. Was that the bhajiwala calling, Vishnu? We have nothing but potatoes.'

Vishnu had risen silently, pulled on his mask and hurried down. He came back with bunches of palak and methi.

'That's all he brings?'

'That's all he brings. Where's Anagha?'

'She was here. Fixed to the TV screen. Now she's in her room. Weeping no doubt.'

'She is seeing the real world for the first time.'

'You've protected her for too long, Vishnu. People have asthma and live tough lives.'

Vishnu had wondered if you could ever protect a young woman too much in this world.

When palak, chapati and dal were served, Anagha had stridden out of her room raging.

'How can this be allowed to happen? You're on

velvet Papa, working for the press. Your salary comes even if the newspaper doesn't. But these people. No work, no money. No money, no food. If they starve and die, it's their business. But it's not really their business, is it? The government sits in Delhi and decides what their business is. Their business is to stay crammed inside their peeling walls. And? And? Starve. Staying indoors cannot be a blanket rule for everybody damn it. People need a window of time to decide for themselves. Give them a week. Give them trains, buses. They've built your city. Those towers of glass and steel. They've served you in your fancy restaurants. Plunged into your sewers to clean your shit. And now you say, stay home without work, without food, the landlord at your door demanding rent…I don't want to eat.'

'If you don't eat, I won't eat,' Vishnu had said.

'Don't. It'll do all of us good not to eat.'

'Not me it won't,' Supriya had responded evenly. 'I need energy to sweep the floor, wash the clothes, clean pots and pans.'

Supriya had begun to eat. The food had gone cold. Anagha had walked off to her room. Vishnu had looked down at his plate and begun to nibble at a chapati. 'I'll step out later,' he had muttered to the silent table. 'There's a crowd of migrants at Bandra station, waiting for a train. Must get some pics.'

Anagha had emerged from her room and switched on the TV again staring at the stream of people on the highway, anxious, walking blindly, their possessions slung on their backs. Children sat astride men's thin shoulders, on the bars of bicycles pushed by their older brothers. Elders sat on handcarts pulled by their sons, or hobbled alongside, their backs bent. Young women walked with stony faces carrying heavy loads on their heads. Some sat by the wayside looking blankly into the distance. Some had put three stones together on the pavement and set something cooking on them, their babies tugging at their breasts.

'Can't bear this,' she had muttered, switching off the TV and getting up. 'Where's Papa?'

'Gone to Bandra station to get pictures.'

'What's happening there?'

'They say a crowd has gathered waiting for a train to come.'

Anagha switched on the TV again. 'There it is, Ma. Look at that crowd.'

'No thanks. I can't afford to sit and weep. I have to keep this house going.'

'That's selfish, Ma.'

'You might say that.' Supriya had swept out of the room into the kitchen.

Anagha had watched the TV coverage of the area outside Bandra station. The crowd was immense, dense, a static human mass held together by hope. The TV reporter, wearing a face mask, was asking the migrants stupid questions.

'Why are you here?'

'Waiting for a train.'

'Where are you going?'

'Gorakhpur.'

'Why are you leaving the city?'

'They say there will be another lockdown.'

'What was your work here?'

'Restaurant.'

'The restaurant has closed?'

'Closed.'

'So no work?'

'No work.'

'Do you think you will manage to get on the train?'

'I'll try.'

'If not?'

'I'll walk.'

'How many kilometres will that be?'

'Don't know.'

'But you will walk?'

'I will walk.'

A posse of policemen had turned up. They announced that there was to be no train. It was a rumour. 'Go home. Don't believe in rumours. Go home,' they urged over their PA system. 'You are not allowed to be out on the street. Go home. There is no special train. No trains are coming. Go home.'

A lone angry voice shouted, 'We are waiting to go home. Give us a train.'

Others joined in. 'Give us a train. Give us a train.'

What they got instead was a lathi charge. The migrants ran for their lives down broad roads, into by-lanes and alleyways, chased by the police doing their duty which was to lay about with their canes where they could, on backs, legs, heads, buttocks. When the street emptied, all that was left behind was footwear strewn across the space in front of the station.

Vishnu returned. 'I couldn't bear to take pictures of the caning and fleeing,' he had said, his head down. 'I took pictures of footwear. And of a little girl crying for her Ma.'

'The girl was lost? And you didn't wait to see what happened to her, Papa? How could you not? Why didn't you bring her home?' Anagha was near to tears.

'Which world do you live in, Anu?' Supriya had demanded impatiently. 'You are twenty-seven. Old enough to know you can't just pick up a child and bring her home.' Anagha glowered at Supriya and turned pointedly to Vishnu.

'How could the mother have left her behind, Papa?'

'She did not leave her behind,' Supriya said. 'The mother was driven away. You saw that.'

Supriya extended a hand and laid it on Anagha's. 'I almost lost you once, Anu. At Dadar station. The earlier train had been delayed. The crowd on the platform was twice as dense as normal. When the late train finally came, the crowd surged forward pushing aside people like us who were waiting for the next train. I was knocked down. I struggled up, but I had lost you. I couldn't see you anywhere in the crowd. I was desperate. Had you been pushed into the train? Onto the tracks? It was only when the train pulled out, and the crowd thinned that I saw you. Tiny, tiny you, standing terrified against the wall of the station far down the platform, wailing your heart out. I hadn't known till then that I could run as fast as I did that day to pick you up and hold you to my heart.'

Supriya squeezed Anagha's hand. 'The girl's mother will come back for her, don't worry. She will not eat, she will not sleep till she has her daughter in her arms.'

'Till then the police will keep her,' Vishnu added. 'They are generally very kind to lost children.' He smiled ruefully.

There was silence. Not an uneasy one, but one that allowed them hope. For the first time in many days, Anagha smiled. 'But I'm not going to sit comfortably under the fan. I have found a way to help, in a ridiculously small but real way. Mostly to make myself feel less selfish, I guess. An NGO is running a food programme for migrants. I have volunteered to help. I'll begin work tomorrow.'

Those were Anagha's last words.

The funeral is desolate. The lockdown has closed all possibilities of human interaction—births, deaths, schools, colleges, offices, factories, autorickshaws, handcarts, taxis, trucks, shops, markets. The city looks abandoned. Only the trees stand in their places.

Nothing more need be said about the events of those days, except that the government came on television to tell the migrants that they had the government's deepest sympathy for their plight. The government was fully aware of the suffering caused by the lockdown. However, there was a silver lining to this passing cloud. They now had the time and the rare opportunity to look inward.

Stink

I'm thinking about life sitting here on the porch. Sometimes I think about life like this. You have to give time to life, to see what's happening, where we're going. Can't be rushing from market to mall to moya to lagin. This tower coming up in front. That's been bothering me. Where they will park? Where they will get water? Anyone knows? Nobody. Grandpa Edwin would have cursed them to narak. I'm not like that. In our family must be genes are going from mother to daughter. I'm sitting here not cursing. Just contemplating. I'm thinking I can't see the setting sun. But then I'm thinking it is setting, no? Same place same time. It doesn't take anybody's komraa to crow and make it rise. It doesn't take anybody's tower to stop it from setting. God's not changing his ways. We are.

This builder must be a repair permissionwala. Proper badmash. All Desmond Baptista's fault grandpa Edwin would have said. Friends they were. Living across the lane, walking to church Sunday morning then stopping off for their toddy. Grandpa came right home after one. Old Baptista stayed on. His father built him the best house in Chuim. But he's drinking toddy and not making a will. What happens? One day he is eating brain masala—oh yes, gets poor Cecilia to make all the richest food—and drooling over the bombil pickle and never looks up. Head falls in plate and he's off. His three boys are at each other's throat. Cedric is a drunk. Father to son genes in that family. So this repair permissionwala slinks in. Must have got Cedric sozzled or something. Buys his share of the house. Cedric only wants cash to drink. He's happy. Builder moves in. He's happy. Some chor in BMC gives him permission to repair. He's happy. But what repair men? That house could have stood for one hundred years more. This repairwala starts banging and the house falls apart. What can other brothers do? Sold out.

That's life.

Look at that cross down the road. Grandpa Edwin put it up. When? 1940. Come '48 cyclone. Blew the tiles off Chuim roofs and uprooted half the coconut trees. Wind rushing at 100 miles per hour men. Five inches rain in one day. Our field flooded up to the knees. All vegetables gone. Only heard stories. God hadn't yet thought of putting me down here. But I can see the cross. It is where it was. Still standing. God blesses us, good days and bad. But we don't deserve Him.

And where does it all lead to? This line of Vernons and Vivians, Rays and Roses, Gavins and Gwens…And now there's Angie's Noel learning to walk and my Cyril, all of sixty-eight, still going on like he was twenty-eight. Luckily not as bad as that fellow Weinstein. But I am afraid. Born same year same month the two of them. I had to read what he had to say for himself. He says when he was growing up—must have been pimply, men—it was the culture. What? Unzipping? He's just found out unzipping is wrong and has gone off to some sex addiction rehab. What use now? He's got twenty women after him. No use telling them sorry for what he made them do yesterday.

When I think coolly, this one of ours isn't like that. Ours wants women to swoon over him and offer themselves. I did that. I swooned over him so bad, it took me years to open my eyes again. He came backstage to congratulate our choirmaster. My first year with the famous Christmas programme. Girls in pink gowns and men in pink waistcoats standing around all sweaty and breathy after the finale. And this one walks in like Konkancha raja. Big man in the community already. We didn't have many big men then. The choirmaster is smiling so hard his face will split. This one says he wants to shake everybody's hands. He does, all twenty hands. He holds mine, looks into my eyes, bends and kisses it. Even now I get goose flesh thinking of it. His hair flops over his eyes. He tosses it back and moves on. 'Well she is our youngest. He's like an uncle,' the choirmaster says afterwards because everybody is shocked and I am red under my make-up. It is true. I am the youngest. Only seventeen. It is true he could be my uncle. But he is not. No uncle ever kissed any niece's hand like that. Then I asked around. Shirley Sequeira knows these things. She says he's big in the community because he's the youngest ever marketing manager in Corn Products. Old American company.

After the kiss, I'm still in a swoon and he's writing little notes to me. He's in Juhu. I'm in Chuim. But he's like that. He's found out my address. He's found a little boy to deliver. And the first note comes. 'Princess of Chuim, your courtier bows to you.' That's it. Another comes a week later. 'Nightingale of Chuim, wish I could hear you in Juhu.' Third week another one. 'Miss Slender Waist, I would happily be your cummerband.' Now he's getting naughty. He writes on pink paper, fine as tulle.

When I think my blood won't rush to my face mentioning his name, I ask my aunt Benita casual like if he is married. If he is, I'm going to tear up all the pink notes. And when the little boy comes, I'm going to send back his note with mine saying 'Write to your wife, not me.' I am brought up proper. I've heard stories about such men. Having one, they want another. Aunt Benita says, '*Naay Babi. Fafetee haay. Aaya vaas gheta taya vaas gheta. Hushar haay pan jada shana.*' My family elders speak our dialect. She's saying he's a butterfly. Sniffs here, sniffs there. He's clever but extra smart.

Well, even at seventeen I'm making sure he's not sniffing at this one. If he's smart, I'm smarter. Girls have to be, no? So I send back a note with the little boy from Juhu, on paper torn from my Davar's notebook—I've joined the secretarial course, miles from home, but where else to go—and this is what my note says. 'I'm a simple Chuim girl. Not smart like Juhu girls. Please do not write to me if you are only sniffing.'

That is very original, he says about the sniffing. He's bowled over, he says. Then he writes, 'I will stop sniffing if you will let me put you in my buttonhole, right next to my heart.' My heart is pounding.

I write back. 'I don't want to be in your buttonhole. I want to be at the altar in Holy Cross Church.' Am I being too bold? I would not say this to his face. But it's easy on paper. I'm dreaming Holy Cross. So why not say it?

I am only a girl taking a chance. He is going to stop writing notes. I'm going to say he was only sniffing. Then I'm going to concentrate on my shorthand and typing. But he comes along asking Pa for my hand. I'm still banging that stiff old typewriter at Davar's. When I come home, there's a storm.

'*Chaghlel ani thukel.*' (Ma)

'*Asaa javaya dokyavar baisnar.*' (Pa.)

'*Thuklyavar tu kaay karshil, pori*?' (Aunt Benita)

They are saying simple things. He'll chew you up and spit you out. This sort of son-in-law will sit on our heads. When he spits you out what will you do, girl? But Auntie is hopeful next minute. 'He's Joseph. She's Maria. If they aren't meant for each other, who is?'

I'm only half listening from the clouds. In my head I'm choosing my gown and veil and bridesmaids. And the band and the date and the ring. I am full of hope and love. Pa puts one condition. She will finish her secretarial course. She will be eighteen then. She will find a job. Then she will marry.

A crazy year follows. He teaches me many things. How to dress. How to eat. How to talk when I meet his friends. I'm bright. Always topped the class. Even at Davar's. I learn fast. One day I dare to say, 'What made you ask?' He looks into my eyes and says, 'Maria my sweetheart, do you even know how beautiful, fresh, charming, pure and intriguing you are?'

He sends me a big bouquet of red roses when I get my first job as a steno. At Voltas. Good company. Good salary. I am eighteen. Pa has to give in. What a wedding we had. My side one dozen aunties in lugras. His side—not much of it, all in America and Australia—in frocks. But when the singing and dancing began, we were all Eastyas together. He said don't wear a gown with a train. You'll spend the wedding worrying about it. So I wore an off-the-shoulder gown with a full skirt, short veil, all tulle. He couldn't take his eyes off me.

Nor I off him. I had never seen anybody so dekhna, like Paul Newman—remember Butch Cassidy?—like that. But floppy hair.

There followed five years of bliss. Dresses and parties, films and food, out every evening with others or just us, holding hands, then making love, love, love. My twenty-fifth birthday I said to him laughing, 'Let's make babies now. Enough of this calendar watching. God put us on earth for that only, no?'

'Don't spoil it now. Why bring God into it?'

'Who am I to bring Him or not bring Him into it? He is in it. He is it, no?'

He looked down at my body and said, 'This is so flawless, so without a blemish. This is what I call God's work. Can we not let it be? Must we tear it apart?'

I said nothing. Only smiled. And lied about my dates. Would he keep count of the turnover at the company or check dates on the calendar at home?

When I got pregnant with Marjorie, he sighed and said, 'Good. I always want you to have what you want.'

'Don't you want what I want?' I asked.

He didn't answer. I wanted at least two more. He chose all the names. They had to have J and M in them. The first was Marjorie, the second was Jerome and the third was Jamie. I didn't want any after that. He said, 'No worries. We have done our duty. God has a solution for us. Abstention.'

I was thirty-five, my waist thirty. He was forty-seven, his middle a paunch. He was calling me Mamma. I was calling him Papa. God was right. It was time to stop. Some go on till their teeth fall out. But we had both had enough.

I had moved from Voltas to Sandoz. I was climbing the ladder at Sandoz. He had become a management consultant with good-good accounts. Not one, not two, but six. I had gone from steno-typist to secretary to the marketing manager. I was speaking proper English. My next promotion was likely to be a leap into the MD's ante-room. He had become a management guru with a formula that made him famous.

'What do you tell those managers?' I asked. I was getting curious about MDs.

He told me his magic formula: EI = C^3+Em.

He looked like he wanted me to ask him what that meant. I asked.

He said, 'EI is emotional intelligence.'

'EI is East Indian first.'

'Was your question serious?'

He gets very polite when he's offended.

'Sorry, it was,' I said. 'That came because I've been reading a lot of stuff about us. About we forgetting who we are and…'

'May I continue?'

'Yes, of course.'

'So emotional intelligence is necessary in business because a leader can't afford to be just smart in the head. He must be smart in the heart. Now, if you are smart in the heart, what are your gains? They are Confidence that comes from self-awareness—that's the first C; Clarity about what you want—that's the second C and ability to communicate what you see clearly—that's the third C. And then there's the final gain of EI—Em, without which the three Cs are inadequate. Em is empathy.'

'Neat,' I said. That pleased him. 'That's how I get old Philomena to make all the wonderful dishes you love.' I shouldn't have added that. He wasn't pleased.

Life is good. The children are doing well. I made it to the MDs ante-room and took early retirement at fifty. I wanted to work for the orphanage. I don't interfere with Joeboy's life. He doesn't interfere with mine. The house is big enough for us. He has his bedroom and his office upstairs. Separate staircase. A feudal Man Friday who'll do anything for him. He comes down sometimes for dinner. Tells Philomena's daughter Della what he wants to eat. We sit together, have a glass of wine, eat, chat and then he's off. I don't ask where he goes. He doesn't tell where he goes. When I have friends over, they ask where's Joe. I say not in my pocket. And we laugh.

It's been going on nicely for years. Then Gracie drives up one day, gives me four sheets of pink paper as fine as tulle, has a cup of tea, a slice of cake and leaves. Gracie is a Vasai girl who's done well in life. I became a steno. She became an air hostess. Flew around for years. Got fed up with the hectic life. Married a foreigner. Dutch, I think. Huisman. Twice her height. Who knows what happened? But a few years later she's back in Bombay with a four-year-old girl and plenty of money in the bank. He must have given her. Those Europeans don't cheat you. Use and chuck. She buys herself a flat in Santa Cruz and settles down taking baking classes and bringing up her daughter. She's good at that. Made my wedding cake before she started flying.

That's really what has set me thinking about life. What do people want? Billions of men and women in the world with billions of dreams and desires. Some ditch them. Some go to death with them. To some, some are granted. What a circus. So what do I do with these sheets of pink paper with one man's undying dreams on them? They are poetic now.

'Candice, incandescent in candlelight
Flames danced in your eyes last night
Your eyes sparkled with azure hue
Where did you get those eyes of blue?
An admirer'

From her father, yedya. Didn't you realise she was Gracie's child from the Dutchman?

'Love is never wrong
Whether short or long
True if momentary,
True through eternity.

An admirer'

Let's keep it short, Joeboy. Face it. You're not a marathoner.

'If I say I love you,
Do not turn away.
For when I looked at you
Your eyes gave you away.
An admirer'

Well, I guess you see what you want to see. Like people who see UFOs.

'A kiss is a thing so gossamer
The buzz of a bee to a flower
Just now I alight
For a moment slight
But promise to come back for more.
An admirer.'

Oh you sad sad fool. You are EI = $B^3 + N^n$. Brashness, Blather, Bullshit + Narcissism raised to 'n'.

I suppose you've found women who fall for this. Don't point to me. You didn't win me with poetry. I'll say I fell for pink paper. But that was then, dear Joey. These days they text and send nude pictures to each other.

I think some more about life and where we have come from, where we are going. What am I supposed to do with these now? I think. I plan. I laugh. It's a dreary business. But if we can get a laugh out of it, it'll be some use. He's coming Sunday night. He wants pork sarpatel. He's already told Della. I was surprised when she told me. Sunday at home for Joeboy? Something wrong there.

He's dapper when he comes. Dark printed shirt tucked in. Despite the paunch. He lowers himself into his favourite chair.

'Before you relax, I want you to do something Papa.'

'Tell and it shall be done Mama.'

'Just sniff around in the kitchen please. I'm getting a stink. Della said no. She's gone. I don't want her to think I didn't trust her. But the stink's been in my nose for two days.'

'Really? What kind of stink.'

'Like a dead mouse. If it is a dead mouse I'll be glad. He's been around nibbling at the potatoes. So I put some Ratgone out. I hate doing that. They eat it and go in a corner and die. And stink up the house. The old mousetraps were good. You remember them? You could let the mouse out alive.'

'See, if there was a dead mouse I'd have smelt it coming down the stairs. You can't hide a dead mouse.'

'Just go around and sniff, Papa. If there's nothing, I'll know it's in my nose. It has probably poked into some dirty business it shouldn't have.'

'Don't be silly. That's one thing you wouldn't do. As a matter of fact, that's your whole problem, Mama. Self-contained. Not interested in the world. You and your job. You and your children. You and your orphanage.'

'First it was I and you. Remember? But I guess you're right. I'm limited. I get by though. With a smile and a tear as they say.'

He hauls himself out of the chair. 'I'll go see. Wild goose chase it will be.'

'And if you smell nothing, can you pick up the Ratgone papers and chuck them in the bin? There's one paper under the sink, one behind the door, one next to the potato basket and one near the fridge.'

'Yes ma'am. At your service ma'am.'

He comes back, sits in the chair and says, 'No mouse. As I thought. The Ratgone is in the bin.'

'Oh good,' I say. He says nothing. I am happy to say nothing. We have a drink. Eat sarpatel. He says nothing. What can he say poor dear. But how long can he hold it, no? He explodes.

'Stink she says. Of course it was in your nose. Of course you poked it where it didn't belong.'

'Perhaps.' I wasn't going to explode, though that's what he wanted.

'Where did you get those from?'

'From Gracie. Mother to Candice. Wife of Huisman. He had blue eyes.'

He slaps his forehead. 'Oh my God. What a fool. What an utter fool. There was nothing to it. I met her…'

'I don't want to know, Papa.'

'Stop calling me Papa.'

'All right. Joey. But remember what the Bible says.

Fornicators along with others like thieves and drunkards will not inherit the kingdom of God.'

'Shut up. That's your other problem. Always quoting the Bible.'

'I live by it.'

'Well I don't. And I don't fornicate, to use your indelicate word.'

'Other things are equally bad these days, sweetheart. I worry for you. Weinstein is in rehab. But big stars are still coming out to tell stories.'

'Weinstein is vulgar. I am not Weinstein. I look for romance in this dreary world. Romance. A beautiful woman is a thing of hope. A dream.'

He gets up and staggers towards the stairs. I turn around to look. He turns around to look.

His face crumples like thin paper in a fist. He sits down slowly on the third step. I stand up and walk to him. His head is buried in his hands. His shoulders are shaking. I sit beside him on the third step and put my arm around them till they stop shaking. Exhausted, he puts his head on my shoulder.

The Swimming Pool

I clambered on to the Shivneri, glad to be in its dry interior. Outside was July rain. Outside was July slush. Outside was quotidian traffic. Shivneris ran from the chaotic traffic into their well-ordered berths under the flyover. Others chugged unhappily out and did not, could not, breathe till they were on the highway, speeding to Pune.

The Shivneri is the pride of the Maharashtra State Transport Corporation. A fully air-conditioned luxury bus, it runs smooth. It brakes with a breathy swoosh. Its doors open automatically with a sigh. It departs on time and arrives on time. Once on the highway, it overtakes the organisation's semi-luxuries, speeds past its red rumblers crammed with the great unwashed, a single question inscribed in their worried eyes: Will the rain reach us in Ahmednagar/Beed/Sholapur/Yavatmal? I look at them and feel a twinge of something like guilt. But what the hell! Did I do anything to make those poor people poor? Nah. So what's my problem?

I store my laptop in the rack above my seat, then take it down again. I admit I can't wrench myself away from it. But I put it up again. I have promised myself that I shall not open it on the ride, not for a single moment. I will look out, observe nature, take in the gleaming trees washed clean by the rain, marvel at the myriad waterfalls streaming down cliff faces, gaze upon slopes covered with succulent grass and wild flowers. In Pune, I will take care to be in the present moment with Siddharth. 'Be in the present moment' is Siddharth's thought for the year. His uncle and hero, Paresh Kaka, has bank notes coming out of his ears and nose. But from his mouth issue wise thoughts which he circulates on the family's WhatsApp group. The family calls him guru and not jocularly either. The family is not given to humour. Their laughter, from what I have noticed, might be better described as sniggering when it is quiet and cackling when it is loud. The family repeat their guru's words of wisdom piously to friends and associates who, in turn, feel blessed. This year, Paresh Kaka has said much about being in the present moment. For example, 'The present moment is the only time when time does not exist. There is neither past nor future in the present. The present is nothing more and nothing less than itself, the present. If you take care of the present, the future will take care of itself and the past will not matter.' When applied to me, the idea of being in the present moment is not to be distracted from the immediate. The immediate is Siddharth and his concerns. There can be no place for a laptop when I'm with him. I carry it with me only because that is what I do. I carry my laptop with me wherever I go. It is now on my lap.

I lean back in my seat. My seat is comfortably cushioned, the curtain across the window and the window itself have been washed clean, allowing me a clear view of the chaos outside. The rain is coming down in sheets. I was lucky to have reached under the flyover before it started. I am as dry as a stick. Unlike the woman who now walks in, squinting up at the seat numbers to find her own. Her drenched sari clings lovingly to her ankles, giving her walk a curious ducklike waddle. She has found her seat. It is next to mine. 'Phew,' she breathes as she places her duffel bag in the rack above and flops down beside me. 'Who told you it's fun going to Pune in the middle of July?' she asks herself and laughs. The question is not meant for my ears. It is meant exclusively for her own. Having asked herself the question, she bends down to squeeze the water out of her sari. Now she has a little pool at her feet. She takes a fluffy hand towel from her capacious turmeric yellow faux patent leather handbag and lays it on the pool. She takes off her slippers and upturns them over the aisle. Droplets of water tumble out and run as far down the aisle as their meagre mass will carry them. She takes another fluffy hand towel out of the same capacious handbag and wipes her feet. 'Don't want to catch cold in this wretched AC.' She is again talking to herself.

I look at the top of her bent head. Her thick, wavy hair is sprinkled lightly with grey. Forty-five? Fifty? She straightens up, leans back and sighs with pleasure. She looks across me out of the window. 'It's July. And the 26th.' Now she looks directly at me to see whether the significance of the date has registered with me. It has. I nod. '2005.'

'Were you caught?'

I shudder. 'Yes. On the Western Express Highway. But near enough to home. I got out of the taxi and walked.'

'My uncle died sitting in his car. He couldn't open his windows to let the air in.'

There are two ways people deal with nightmare memories. They never mention them. Or they mention them each time an occasion presents itself.

'I'm looking forward to the Khopoli batata wada,' I say to lighten things between us. It is a stupid non-sequitur as non-sequiturs go. But she doesn't seem to think so. She looks at me with interest.

'Oh? You'll get down at the food mall?'

'Of course. Won't you?'

'I will have to.' She holds up her little finger in explanation. 'But I won't stop to eat and drink. Always scared the bus will leave without me.'

'That doesn't happen. We waited half an hour once for a man who had got into an argument with a stranger and forgotten about the bus. After several announcements, his neighbour, the only one who remembered what he looked like, got off, looked for him, found him arguing and hauled him back, still raving and ranting.'

My neighbour laughed. Then laughed some more.

'You go to Pune often?'

'Every Sunday.' Then, in answer to a question she hadn't asked and which I could easily have left unanswered, I said, 'To see my mother.'

'Umm,' she said, full of understanding. But I could see she was preparing to ask me something else. I braced myself for it. Are you married? How many children do you have? Instead, she said with what looked like a naughty smile, 'Could you fetch me a vada with yours?' She was clearly salivating. 'Look at me! No shame!'

The man at the counter barely glanced at me. He was used to my weekly face and my order of one plate vada without chutney. I'd had chutney the first time around and sat with my tongue hanging out. 'Here. Have a pinch of this. Best cure after that chutney,' my neighbour had said, proffering an open packet of sugar.

Now, standing before the counter, I had to shout 'Two' twice over before the man looked at me with a question creased vertically on his forehead. 'Two,' I repeated through the din.

'Two no chutney?'

I dithered. I hadn't asked. The man had no time for ditherers. He served me two with no chutney. I would normally have eaten my vada piping hot, standing before the counter. But I rushed back to save my neighbour from getting jittery. Also, to ensure that she too had her vada hot.

She liked it. Actually, loved it. 'Sorry I didn't get chutney. I find it too hot.'

I saw the saliva gather in her mouth. 'It's okay. Next time.'

'It's very hot.'

'Some like it hot.' She grinned, making sure I noticed she had said something naughty.

'You've seen the film?'

She nodded, her mouth full of vada. 'DVD. My husband and I used to watch old films. Our Akshay was at IIT. Our Ashwini was at NID. There was time. But that was before your time. Back then we used to have these DVD players. All you did was…'

'I'm not that young you know.' I hadn't wanted to sound rueful. But I suspect I did. I instantly undid the effect by crumpling up my vada wrapper nonchalantly, stuffing it into the plastic bag I carried for the purpose and offering a cliché. 'But what the hell. Age is only a number.'

She sighed. 'Not really. You feel it in your bones. I feel it in the water. Maybe because I've only just started again.'

I looked at her.

'Swimming,' she explained.

'Where do you swim?'

'Tilak talav.'

'Where's that?'

'Deccan Gymkhana.'

'In Pune?'

'Yes. Just off Prabhat Road. You don't have to be a member. Just pay and dive in.'

'I got the impression you lived in Mumbai.'

'I do. I do. But I swim in Pune.'

She grinned at my bewildered expression. 'Simple. It's because my husband loves me. He was determined I should swim. He always says, love is not love unless it is based on respect. I respect your wishes. You wish to swim. You shall swim. He was a professor in a government college. He speaks like that.'

I continued to look bewildered. She thought I had not understood her husband's definition of love. She elaborated. 'There's love that happens before marriage. It might lead to marriage and then it might not. I don't know. I didn't have it. My husband also didn't have it. We had love after marriage. That means we began as strangers. Then we got used to each other. Then we began to trust each other. I looked after his parents till the day they died. He worked hard through all his transfers and got promoted from lecturer to professor when it was time. He is a great believer in the Bhagvad

Gita. He says there are two things we must live by. Nishkam karma and observe your dharma. Both of us do that. Do your work. Don't expect fruit. And do what you were born to do. Don't waver. That's why we have never needed to argue. We have given the children a peaceful home to grow up in. They are doing well. My husband too was earning well by the time he retired. All those Pay Commissions.

'Then my rheumatism started. I said one day let's hire a cook. My wrist hurts when I stir the pot and roll the chapatis. My husband said to the children that night at dinner, "Your mother would like to keep a cook. What do you think?" They both wailed. "No Aai. No cook please. Cooks make awful chapatis." My husband looked at me with…umm…devotion. When he looks at me like that, I know what's coming. It came. "And your aamti. How much love you put into it! Which cook will do that?" Then he did something that is typical of him. He looked for consensus and compromise. He said to the children, "Forget cooks. But don't you think Aai deserves some help in the kitchen? What if we hired someone to do her cutting and chopping and kneading and that sort of thing?" The children thought it an excellent idea. "That would help, wouldn't it?" he said, turning to me. I was grateful. Even to have someone in the kitchen with me to…It would stop me from…'

There was a long pause. I didn't want to break it. There are things people don't want to say even to strangers on a train. Or, in this case, a bus. I was about to turn away to take in the view of the approaching hills that we would soon drive into, when she quickly said, 'from...from...talking to myself.' She gave an embarrassed giggle and looked at me for some sign that said it was absolutely okay to talk to oneself. Perhaps my expression told her that. So back she went into top gear even as the bus driver shifted into low to negotiate the ghat. 'So now I have Kunda, not just the pots and pans, to talk to,' she said merrily. 'When my mother-in-law was alive...'

I drifted away. I didn't want to hear about her mother-in-law. Or her husband. Or her children. I have no patience with families. Not mine. Not Siddharth's. Not anybody's. What I did want to know was why a middle-aged woman who lived in Mumbai went to Pune to swim. How could I prompt her to return to that?

I waited till she was done with her mother-in-law and quickly said, 'Swimming is supposed to be good for rheumatism, isn't it?' I couldn't have hit the nail harder on the head. She nodded vigorously. 'Not just good. It is very good for rheumatism. My husband's doctor friend, whom he admires and trusts, told him so. My husband mentioned it to me casually at the dinner table. I grabbed at the idea. Toning down my enthusiasm—no point tempting fate—I pushed as gently as I could. "Perhaps we could try it. Nothing else is helping."

'Luckily the children too chipped in. "It's the best cardio there is. Involves the total body." Akshay.

'"You'll lose all your flab. We'll have a new you." Ashwini.

'"Best stress buster too." Akshay.

'"Just think. We are rushing around worrying about exams and job prospects, and you're lying back in the water letting the cares of the world float away." Ashwini.

'My husband was happy the children approved of his idea. "But you'll have to start learning," he said, a little worried. "Perhaps you are too old for that?"

Here my neighbour turned to me. Did she wink? I'm not sure. But her expression suggested a wink. 'I didn't let on that I used to swim like a fish before marriage.'

'You did? And he didn't know?'

'In my time, when the boy's side came to see the girl, they asked things like can you thread a needle, to check that you didn't secretly wear glasses. And can you make pohe, to check your family hadn't fibbed about your culinary skills. Nobody asked me if I could swim. How could I butt in and say I can also swim? And once we were married, the subject never came up.'

'But you could actually swim like a fish?'

'Oh yes. A school friend and I. She took part in races and won medals. She used to urge me to race. So did our coach. But I didn't want to race. I just wanted to be in the water and feel it ripple on my skin. My friend became the national champion. And I became the national housewife.'

I was about to commiserate with her when I noticed she wasn't being either ironic or rueful. She was laughing. So, I nipped my sympathy in the bud and waited. She had grown thoughtful.

'Yes. That's what I enjoyed. The feel of the cool water on my skin. Lying on my back looking up at the sky. Sometimes colourless. Sometimes colourful. But always with birds gliding across it. Fascinating how they'd suddenly stop flapping their wings and simply glide. I'm on my back, floating. They are up there gliding. Am I thinking? No. Are they? No. We are just…just being. Following our dharma.'

'Where was this? I mean where did you live?'

'Oh, didn't I tell you? Pune. My friend and I swam in the Tilak tank. Imagine, it will soon be a hundred years old.'

'The Tilak tank?'

'The same. They say Sir Dorabji Tata wanted to send our swimmers to Antwerp for the Olympics and stood behind the whole…'

'Where do you live in Mumbai?'

'Hindu Colony.'

'The Mahatma Gandhi swimming pool is just across the bridge. Isn't it less trouble going there?'

'Look. Here's Lonavala. Will you be getting off at this food mall too?'

'No. We can continue talking.'

'I don't want to bore you.'

'You're not boring me. Honest.'

'Sure? Okay. Then very quickly. My husband went to the MGMO to find out about membership and coaching. The pool was closed because of some leaks. When we heard it had opened, my husband went to enrol me. But it had closed again. Some filtration problem. Then it closed a third time because its outer wall got washed away or something. By then my husband was fed up and said let's forget about swimming. Let's try homeopathy. That night…you know how it is with men…you give something you get something. So, after I did my dharma, I said what about Tilak tank? Where is that he muttered, tired from the exercise. I said Pune. He half heard. I said, "Icouldtakeamorningbusandbebackbynight." His breathing had got heavier. I said, "Onceamonthsundayswhatdoyousay?" He mumbled something. I said "Thank you. I'll cook lunch and dinner before I leave. Kunda will make tea. You can order snacks, no? So that's fixed."

'When I got home the first Sunday, my husband was very upset.

'"Where were you the whole day? We were so worried."

'"I left you a note. I knew you'd forget."

'"The note said something about swimming."

'"That's what I was doing."

'"Swimming? Where? Whatever for?'

'"Tilak tank. For my rheumatism."

'I pampered him and Akshay and Ashwini the rest of the month. And here I am again. I've left my husband a note to say the chapatis are in the dabba. There are two veggies and aamti in the fridge. Kunda will serve them.'

She sighed a long luxurious sigh and leaned further back in her seat. 'What about you? Where do you live in Mumbai?'

'Bandra.'

'And you go to see your mother every Sunday?'

'What? Oh yes. Yes.'

'How nice for her. My mother died eight years ago. Of shock. Because my father died.'

'I'm sorry.'

'I'm over it now. We're like water. A stone drops in. The water ripples around it for a while then turns placid again. Healed.'

We were almost at Parihar Chowk. I shuffled.

'Where does your mother live?' she asked.

'Mother? Oh yes...yes. Baner.'

'You should get off at Wakad. Much closer.'

'I know. But my mother likes jalebis from a halwai here. I always carry a quarter kilo for her.'

'No diabetes hunh?'

'Luckily not.'

She stood up in the aisle to let me go.

'Have a great swim,' I said.

'Enjoy the jalebis,' she said.

Sidhharth was waiting to pick me up. We drove down the leafy Pashan Road to his flat. As always, he had ordered in food. As always, it was vegetarian pizza. No fuss. Quick to eat. Easy to clean up after.

The bed too was ready. We ate, we made love, we snoozed. We walked down the road to our favourite Udipi for filter coffee. This woke us up. He told me about his week at work. He was in IT. I told him about my week at work. I was with a placement agency. He was not in the present moment. He was playing jalatarang with his spoon on the rim of his cup. I was angry. I hated his jalatarang. But we weren't married. I didn't have to live with it. He hated my taking the Shivneri. He thought I should take an Uber. But again, we weren't married. We could call it quits anytime we wanted. He heard my silence, put down his spoon and sighed, 'What else?'

I told him about the woman on the bus.

At the end of my story, he picked up his spoon again and, holding it poised over his cup, said, 'You believed all that?'

'I beg your pardon?' My voice was as cold as I could make it.

'You thought that was the real story? Coming to Pune to swim in Tilak tank?'

I narrowed my eyes and looked at him. He had a large nose.

'Is that what you are doing in Pune?' he continued. 'Swimming in Tilak tank?'

My blood shot up suddenly from normal to boiling point. But I said nothing. The waiter was giving us dirty looks. There were a dozen people waiting outside to get in. Siddharth paid and we left.

We returned to his flat in absolute silence. Once home, we had an all-out row. It had been waiting to happen. Two years is a long time for a weekly roll in the hay. Inflammable stuff, hay. A spark falls and there's a conflagration.

'You're such a cynical shit,' I said casually.

'Where did that come from?'

'That woman came to Pune to swim.' My voice echoed around the flat it was that loud.

'So?'

'So, you had no business laying your dirty paws on her.'

From here we went on to do better and better. He told me how he hated my this, that and the other. I told him how I hated his this, that and the other. He dragged in my family. I dragged in his. And then I said what I had been dreaming of saying for ages. 'This is the end.' To which he said, 'I f***ing agree.'

Then we flung the 'f' word at each other in all its forms, tenses and declensions—noun, adverb, adjective, present participle, past participle, the lot. Exhausted, we walked down to his car. I felt lighter than I had felt for a long time. He dropped me off at Parihar Chowk. He didn't wait till my bus came. I spotted the woman as soon as I got in. 'God, let my seat not be the empty one next to hers.' It was. She greeted me like a long-lost friend. I needed silence. I received human warmth.

'I hope your mother is well.'

'Oh yes she is.'

'I'm so glad you caught this bus. I was hoping you would. Now I'll treat you to sabudana khichadi at Datta's. In return for this morning's batata vada.'

'You mean we will get off together and have it sitting in the restaurant?'

'Yes, of course.'

'You're not afraid of missing the bus?'

'Not here. Not at Datta's. This is like home.'

'Maybe the swim calms you down.'

'That it does. It's a lovely pool.'

I looked out at the pouring rain. 'From water to water.'

'I know. It's such fun. Little coronets dancing all around you. And cloudy elephants above, bringing the sky closer.'

My WhatsApp pinged. Siddharth. 'If your swimmer friend is on the bus, ask her if she has a niece or something. I'm looking for someone who cooks and cares.'

'She says they don't make them like her any more. She also suggests you try fucking yourself.'

'No need to do that. Where I come from, they're making her kind by the sackful. Ba has lined up a few for me. Maybe I'll go pick one.'

'Bastard.' I switched off.

'There it is,' my neighbour said happily. 'Datta's.'

The Bhikbali

'We say about a stinking rich man that he has enough money to feed seven generations without their having to lift a finger.' Vishwajit reclined in his chair. It creaked. The city was under lockdown and there was more time to share his bitterness with his wife than he had ever had.

Aruna nodded. She knew where this opening line was leading. She was snapping the heads and tails off French beans, stringing them and putting them in a colander to be chopped and washed later. There was no hurry. Her office was closed. She didn't have to cut Vishwajit short because she had to rush through chores. She could let him talk. It made him feel good. That made her feel good. These were peaceful times. Mother-in-law was away in Pune, staying with her younger son, stuck there because of the sudden lockdown.

Ashu and his family had settled in Detroit. He was a doctor, she a physiotherapist. They had made a video call last evening. The latest figures for Detroit were 4000 cases, 130 deaths. Please be careful, Vishwajit had said. Please be careful, Aruna had said. Ashu had said, don't worry. It's only hitting the poor.

'Like that bus driver. We read about him in the newspaper,' Aruna said.

Vishwajit said, 'You're living in a developed country. Not like us uneducated lot. Why did that woman sneeze all over that bus driver without covering her nose? Poor fellow died.'

'He was old,' Ashu said stiffly. His voice made it clear he wanted to hear no more criticism of his adopted country or its people. The conversation ended. No use worrying about Ashu. What will worry do? Someone on TV had said worry lowers your immunity. We don't want to lower ours. Vishwajit and Aruna had agreed on that.

'We say about a stinking rich man that he has enough money to feed seven generations without their having to lift a finger.' Vishwajit reclined in his chair. It creaked. 'I had an ancestor who was filthy rich. I'm the seventh generation from him. I'm working my a**e off to keep body and soul together.'

'Me too.'

'What?'

'Working that thing off.'

'When I say me, I include you.'

Aruna snaps a bean. 'Ashu's doing well.'

'Not because of the grand old man. Because of this poor chawl-dweller.'

'I suppose that includes me.'

Vishwajit was not amused. A quick change of subject was required but not too far from the present line of conversation or he would think she wanted to change the subject and be even less amused. 'We really must clean out the loft one of these days. So much junk has piled up there since your great-great-grandfather moved from the hill to the plains.'

'Great-great-great grandfather. He's the one who moved down. You've seen the house, haven't you?'

'Once. Mother-in-law insisted I should. To see what a grand family we were. We went by bus, then climbed up a snaky path, she with her knees, huffing, puffing and laughing. There it is, she kept saying every now and again. Then, no not that.'

'So, it still stands.'

'Did. Twenty-five years ago.'

'She told you lots of stories about us, didn't she? Family stories always travel down from one generation of women to the next. The kitchen was full of chatter when you first came. You couldn't have been talking about your office. What did she tell you?'

'Oh all sorts of things.' Aruna gave him an arch look. She used to do that in the early years. He had forgotten the look. Something stirred in him.

'Stop playing hard to get,' he said, smiling a rare smile.

'But I am hard to get, saheb,' she said. 'I can't sit chatting. I have to cook dinner.'

'Saheb?' A tingle ran up his spine. She used to call him that on 'special' occasions. 'Come on now. Stop teasing. There's plenty of time for dinner.'

'Ok. Let me just wash these and come.'

Aruna got up with the colander of stringed French beans and turned to go in. He watched her back. Twenty-five years and she had not changed much. The same curves give or take a few kilos. He remembered that back from their 'seeing' ceremony in the small sitting room of her parents' home in Prabhadevi. She had risen from her chair to fetch dishes of pohe from the kitchen. He had noticed a slender waist flaring into full buttocks, a thick braid of glossy hair swinging across them as she walked. He had read descriptions of female backs in novels. He was seeing a real one now. After that vision, he had not paid much attention to the bright yellow pohe she had placed in his hand, garnished with shavings of white coconut and fresh green coriander leaves.

Her mother had said, 'Our Aru is an excellent cook,' adding self-deprecatingly, 'Which is more than my mother could have said about me when he came to see me.' She cast a sideways glance at her husband who sat in a corner looking at his nails. 'We lived in a bungalow in Juhu back then. He came to see me there. Remember?' Her husband nodded at her look. 'My father was a film producer. We had two servants and a cook. Why would I need to cook? But…' She smiled a sad smile, waiting for Vishwajit's mother to ask 'But what?'

Vishwajit's mother asked, 'But what?'

Aruna's mother said, 'You know what the film line is like. My father put a lot of money in a film that sank without a ripple.'

A melancholy silence followed, which it was all right for Vishwajit's mother to break since she was breaking only the silence, not the mood. 'I know how that must have felt. Vishu's great-great-grandfather lived on Malabar Hill. A big man. A really, really big man. But he lost all. Everything. On the stock market.'

Had she missed a couple of greats? Things got a little confusing after two. Her husband had told her to count three before grandfather. But you can't talk and count at the same time. Anyway, beyond two, it gets boring. She had carefully avoided looking at her husband after this public foray into family history.

'In a way then, our children were born for each other,' Aruna's mother had said brightly. Vishwajit's mother had pressed her lips together in a tight line, her expression saying, 'You forward woman! We might reject your daughter all the same.'

Vishwajit did not want 'boy's side' power play to stand between him and this girl with a back that only novelists could describe.

'It does look as though we were,' he said with a bold look at Aruna. A sweet smile had emerged at the corner of her lips.

That sealed it. The wedding followed soon after and Aruna became a rightful heir to the Grand Ancestor Story of which Vishwajit had inherited the male side and Aruna the female. Vishwajit did not have a head for history. He loved mythology. But in this case, he had every historical detail down pat. When Aruna returned from the kitchen minus colander, he said, 'Before you tell me what my mother told you, let me tell you what my father told me.'

Aruna smiled encouragingly.

Vishwajit sat forward in his chair. 'The ancestor's name was Narhari Govind. Did you know that?'

Aruna shook her head.

'There was a cotton boom in Bombay that started in 1861. Did you know that?'

Aruna shook her head.

'Our ancestor was a share broker. Did you know that?'

Aruna shook her head. 'Please assume I know nothing. I'm already bored.'

Vishwajit smiled, reclined in the chair and took off like an express train.

'America was fighting a civil war over slavery. Britain needed cotton for its mills in Lancashire and Manchester. India replaced America as its source for cotton. Narhari Govind put his savings into the cotton trade. Bombay was growing. It was getting overcrowded. More land was needed. The government decided to reclaim the Back Bay. It set up a company called the Backbay Reclamation Company. A lakhpati named Premchand Roychand bought most of the shares and floated other companies whose shares smaller punters bought. Narhari Govind was one of the smaller punters. Shares were going at four times their face value. Imagine, at its peak, shares were Rs 55,000 apiece. Narhari Govind bought and sold, bought and sold. Couldn't stop the money rolling in. He built himself a palatial bungalow on Malabar Hill and lived like a king. Then tragedy struck. On 18 April 1865, he along with other speculators heard the terrible news. The American Civil War had ended and with it the cotton boom. The share market collapsed. Entire fortunes were wiped out, among them our ancestor's. The Backbay Reclamation had to end at Marine Drive. Only Roychand survived the crash. Narhari Govind died of shock. His son Vishnu Narhari sold off the mansion on Malabar Hill and moved to Nana Chowk. We went further and further downhill till my grandfather moved to this chawl.'

Aruna was shocked. So that is how it had happened. The story left Vishwajit bitter again. Aruna noticed and said brightly, 'Don't you want to hear my story now?'

'It's not a fairy tale, is it? The end cannot change.'

'No, it can't. But this story isn't about the end or cotton or stocks and shares.'

Like Vishwajit, who had heard the grim facts of the story several times from his father and had it down pat, Aruna had heard the bright facts within the grim story enough number of times from her mother-in-law to have them down pat.

'She used to call him just He. So I'll do the same.'

'Who used to call whom?'

'Your mother, your ancestor.'

'Narhari Govind.'

'Yes. Him.'

'She didn't know his name?'

'I don't know. What she knew was his style. First his clothes. At home He wore a fine muslin dhoti with a broad red border. Mother-in-law said His dhotis were so fine you could see…she never completed the sentence.' Aruna gave Vishwajit her newly recovered arch look. 'She didn't need to. She knew I knew what she meant.'

'Really! You women!'

'With the fine-spun dhoti went a loose white coat, always freshly laundered. It had twelve ties down the front. When He went out, He wore a black coat cut in the European style, a dazzling white shirt whose high collar and cuffs showed at the neck and wrists, narrow white trousers, black European style shoes, a red pagdi and in one ear what Mother-in-law called a bhikbali.'

'A bhikbali?'

'Yes. A tiny gold ring that He wore in the upper

ear she said. It was set with two real, not cultured pearls, with one large ruby and one small emerald drop hanging from it. She said He cut a magnificent figure. His chest used to be bare when He sat down to breakfast and dinner on a low stool with carved silver corners, covered only by a richly bordered shoulder cloth. That's when you saw the gold band around his arm. Mother-in-law said His wife who sat before him on the floor serving him the dishes that the servant brought in, could never take her eyes off that arm although she saw it twice every day, at breakfast which was at ten before He left for the office and in the evening at dinner which He had after his puja. Both meals were served on a large silver plate which was so heavy his wife could not lift it with one hand. There were three silver bowls on the plate, one for dal, one for fish curry and one for the sweet. His wife would pour water into his silver tumbler from an ornamental silver water pitcher. Mother-in-law always stopped here and asked, do you think it was easy to lift that pitcher?'

'Wasn't it?' I asked. I knew it wasn't. But I wanted to hear her say why.

'Of course it wasn't,' she laughed. "That water pitcher wasn't one of our thin steel things. Oh no. It was two or three kilos of pure silver. Remember, the wife wasn't lifting only the pitcher. She had to lift her own arm to lift the pitcher. On her wrist were half-a-dozen thick gold and pearl bangles weighing a quarter kilo each.

That was when she was at home. When she went to weddings in her heavy kasbi sari, she wore kangans, ruiphulas and pichodis on her wrists, khelnas on her arms, a thick surry and other pieces around her neck, a gold flower veni around her high bun…oh my god. Can you imagine the vision? She must have looked like the goddess Lakshmi herself.'

Aruna drew a deep breath for the third part of the story.

'While He was at breakfast, His vehicle would be waiting for him outside—a British-made landau drawn by two magnificent white horses. Two footmen in livery rode in the back. The coachman in livery sat on the box up front. Only the servant riding on the footboard was poorly dressed as servants should be. Mother-in-law said when the landau rode through the streets of Girgaum, people crowded the balconies of chawls to gawp at the sheer splendour of the man.'

They were about to finish dinner, when a crack of thunder split the sky.

'Rain,' Vishwajit said gloomily.

'Looks like it,' Aruna rose with the dinner plates. Vishwajit followed her to the kitchen.

'Why are you here?' she said.

'That room's too silent without you.'

'It just thundered. That's plenty of noise.'

'I don't want noise. I want sound. Where is that two-in-one we used to have? And the cassettes?'

'Everything that's not here is in the loft.'

'Come. Let's go up. You said it needs cleaning.'

'We need daylight.'

'For what? For being together?'

'What's wrong with you? We are together here.'

'This is not our space. Our space is up there. Was. Once.'

Aruna turned from the sink to give Vishwajit a look that turned from hard to amused.

'Don't you remember what Father said on our first night? That's your bedroom up there. That's the best I could do for you. Up you go. He was very naughty.'

'Like son, like father,' Vishwajit said, his hand on her back, his eyes on her mouth forming an 'o' round 'naughty'.

'But he never talked about old family wealth, like you.' Aruna allowed his hand to stay.

Vishwajit withdrew his hand and frowned. 'Yes, he didn't.'

'He once said to me…'

'…what our ancestors could do they did. What we could do, we have done. We have been government clerks. Nothing bad about that.'

'Those were his words.'

'Let's forget him. He puts me in a bad mood. Come.'

'Where?'

Suddenly playful, Vishwajit sang the opening lines of an old stage song: *Come hurry my love come hurry/ To the room above, don't tarry.* His hand was on her back again, urging her out of the kitchen.

'So much junk,' Vishwajit said looking around the loft.

'Open this bag.' Aruna pushed an old scuffed leather suitcase towards him. He opened it and drew out of its dark depths little jhablas and bonnets and triangular nappies and quilted spreads and a square piece of rubber cloth. 'What's all this?'

'Your first month's clothes,' Aruna giggled. 'Mother-in-law had kept them for your brother. But that brother never came. The clothes stayed in the bag till our Ashu was born. She showed them to me for the first time then. Ashu wore them.'

'Ashu wore what I had worn? And you kept them for...'

'Nobody.' Aruna tossed her head.

'It's not too late. You can still...'

'You're mad.'

'I am, I am.' Vishwajit was looking at her through half-closed eyes in the brash light of the single hanging bulb.

Aruna drew his attention hastily to the rest of the junk.

'We must throw all this out,' he said with a grand

sweeping gesture. 'We must reclaim our space.'

'You think Mother-in-law will allow it?'

Vishwajit opened a notebook from a stack bound together by a strip of cloth.

'Look here. Rice was 4 annas a sher. Mother had stored one maund of it in 1950.'

'How much for how much did you say?'

Vishwajit whipped out his phone and Googled, 'sher'.

'Sher was just under 1 kg…4 annas was our 25 paise. One maund is 40 sher…that's about 35 kg. So we ate 35 rupees worth of rice in 1950.'

'Stored in that bin, see? We used it later to store water. When it sprang holes it came up here.'

'And that thing next to it…what is that?' Vishwajit looked at her, his light eyes twinkling significantly behind his brown-rimmed glasses. He looked handsome, Aruna thought.

'You know the answer. Why ask?'

'Because I want you to say it. Come on say it.' He threw his head back, laughing. 'Look at you. All of forty-five and blushing.'

'Rubbish. I never blush,' she said, walking to a small tin trunk in the corner.

'What's that?'

'Open it. I know what's in there.'

Vishwajit opened the trunk. Its latch was stiff but it gave with a good heave.

'That's Mother-in-law's nine-yard kasbi sari. I have worn it to many weddings. That's her visiting one. Father-in-law got it for her from Sholapur, she said. And that…that is for you to see.'

Vishwajit drew out from the far corner of the trunk a little carved box inlaid with ivory. Inside it, on a bed of maroon velvet lay a bhikbali, its pearls, ruby and emerald gleaming softly in the light of the bulb.

'Is it…no. It can't be.'

'It is.'

'His?'

'Yes. Preserved over…how many years?'

'If we're counting from His death in 1890, then 130 years.'

'Mother-in-law had hoped that one day you would strike gold like Him and wear the heirloom.'

'Poor simple woman.'

'Mothers have dreams for their sons.'

'So that is why she had my upper ear pierced. She insisted I wear a cumin seed stalk in the hole to keep it open. I didn't bother.'

'It might still be open. Shall we try?'

Aruna slipped the gold wire from its clasp. It had a fine point made to enter the minutest hole. She felt Vishwajit's upper ear for the hole, found it and said, 'Ready? I'm going to do it quickly. If it goes in, cheers. If not…that's that. Ready?'

'H'm.'

Aruna threaded the wire through the hole. It went in like a needle through butter.

'That's a miracle.'

'What?'

'The hole's open.'

'So put the ring in.'

'It's in. Let me secure the clasp. Now look.'

Aruna pulled out from the trunk a rectangular wooden box.

'Mother-in-law's kumkum box,' she explained. Opening it and placing the hinged mirror on the edge of the box, she said, 'Look at yourself. just look.'

Vishwajit bent low to catch his image in the sloping mirror. It had lost its mercury in patches. But shifting his head a little, he saw his upper ear adorned with the bhikbali.

'He kept a mistress. She lived somewhere in these parts.'

'Who?'

'He.'

'No, He didn't. He was an upright man.'

'He was a rich man. Mother-in-law said all rich men kept mistresses.'

'Mother said that?'

'She did. Imagine the scene. This magnificent man walks in, reclines against the bolsters and asks for paan. She makes it up for him with slow, seductive movements. He insists on her feeding it to him. She bends forward…'

Vishwajit was feeling very strange. 'I'm going to change,' he said, rising. His step was already on the ladder when he turned, walked to the mattress standing next to the bin and unrolled it. He pulled the silk saris out of the tin trunk. He draped one over Aruna's shoulder. He spread another on the mattress. Then, without a word, he descended.

When he came up again, he was wearing a dhoti, a sheer mulmul kurta and the bhikbali. He was a very very rich man. Aruna had thrown the peacock blue sari around herself, switched off the light bulb and lit an old oil lamp. She had found the two-in-one and a langorous male voice was singing *Barsan laage re badariya savan ki rutu kari kari*: The clouds have burst, the rain comes down. How dark is the season, oh how dark. *Chamki chamki bijuriya chamke.* Lightning flashes, flashes again.

The song went on. Thunder rumbled overhead. The rain came crashing down.

Daybreak Over the Gandaki

I was standing there.

I was standing there looking down.

I was standing there looking down at the water far below.

The water far below was grey.

I looked up at the sky.

The sky was grey.

There was no sun. There was water.

The water was grey.

I drew a breath. My breath was shallow. I was dry inside. The twig of an old tree.

I looked at my hands. Dry. My hands, unrecognisable.

But attached to me.

I put them on the railing. The railing was hot. Blistering. I curled my fingers around it. I gripped it hard.

My knuckles white.

Inside my head was all white.

I took my hands off the rails.

I tried to breathe deep. My breath was shallow.

I saw his pinched face. He had little breath left.

I heard him. 'Mamma, Ajji will be there to hug me?'

I moaned. I remembered and I moaned. I stepped up on the ledge of the bridge.

I leaned over and closed my eyes.

I hoisted myself up.

I was hanging half over like an empty petticoat on a clothesline. The railing bit into my waist. I lifted my feet off the ledge.

A hand gripped my ankles. Another reached up to my waist. I was hauled back.

A voice said close to my ear, 'You should see this bridge from Dadar beach. It is magical.'

I screamed.

I was on my back. I was looking up at a blur of white.

I heard whispers. Faint music.

My tears would not stop.

For days and days, my tears did not stop.

I wrote this down months later. Part of my therapy. Pulling out of my memory one jagged shard after another, drawing blood as they came. Write it, he said. Then read it. Write it then read it. The edges grow blunt. Hold it up to your face. Face it. Recite it to yourself. Constantly. The pain will dull. Let it dull till it dulls to nothing.

The doorbell rings. My caregiver answers it. Avinash enters in his quiet way and sits on the chair across from me. The fading sun strokes his glossy hair with soft fingers.

Avinash comes every evening. He does not come to cheer me up as others do. He comes to wait patiently for the day I will say, yes tell me your story. I have not said it yet, for then I must tell him mine. That is the deal. That is the therapy. I am not sure I have the strength to do it. He doesn't push me. He waits. And he talks of other things. The world of men bothers him. Their vanity, their murderous will to power. Women must not kill themselves, he says. The world needs them. He speaks of an arresting image from a film he has recently seen.

'Who did you go with?' I ask for something to say.

'Nobody,' he answers. 'With myself. I am not ready for company. I am working on my breath. Making it come up free and clear, with no hidden sob.'

❧

It is raining hard. The first shower. The rail I gripped must be sizzling.

'Let's go to Dadar beach. You said the bridge looks magical from there.'

My caregiver is happy. She hands me my dupatta.

Avinash drives down the broad avenue at a

controlled speed. I shut my eyes. I cannot take the sight of so much metal whizzing by.

'Papa Landrover. Papa Merc. Papa BMW. Papa look look look. Ferrari.' Tear drops gather behind my eyelids.

'Open your eyes, Mrs Patil.'

'I can't.'

'Try.'

I open my eyes. The teardrops slide down, leaving a mist behind. I cannot see much now.

Soon it is the sea. Not pretty. No sand. No beach. I lift my eyes. The Sea Link stands solid against the grey sky, misted over by the rain, its cable stays sloping gracefully in deceptively delicate fans. I gasp. Then turn around. I don't want beauty. Beauty is false. It is wrong. Morally wrong. Gentle hands turn me around. The voice says, 'Face it.' I hate that voice. I want silence around me. And all the ugliness the world can throw at me. I cross my arms. I dig my nails into my upper arm. I draw blood.

'Let's go,' he says. 'You've done enough for the day.'

As always, before leaving, Avinash says, 'Can I come tomorrow? Or do you want to be left alone?'

Earlier I would say, desperately, 'Please, please come.' Then I would nod dully and say 'Okay', and he would say 'Okay what? Come or you want to be alone?' Then I began to say, 'So much trouble for you. I'll manage.' And he would say, 'I'd rather come here than sit at home alone. But not if you want to be alone.'

And I would say, 'I don't want to be alone.' And he would come.

Today I say, 'Why do you ask? I get through an evening when you come.' Then I look out of the window at the sibilant rain. 'Do you want a hot cup of tea before you go?'

'Half a cup would be nice,' he says. My caregiver makes one cup. I have the other half.

Kishor had been talking nostalgically about the Irani cafe round the corner from his college where he used to go for cutting chai and khari every evening with the boys.

'Why do you call it cutting chai papa? What does the chai cut?'

A sudden sob. Avinash looks up at the sound. My cup rattles in the saucer. He puts down his cup and steadies mine.

I am embarrassed. 'He once asked his father what cutting chai meant. Did it cut something? Kishor said the meaning is in the tasting. I'll take you one day to have a cup.'

'What does cutting chai mean?' I ask involuntarily. I am embarrassed. 'Sorry. I…'

Avinash smiles. He rarely smiles. 'I'll tell you what it means. This half cup we are having. One cup cut in two. That's what it is. The Irani has no patience with grammar. But he doesn't want to be rude. Ek cut chai sounds abrupt. Rude. Ek cutting chai. That sounds rounded, welcoming. Like come-in chai.'

I laugh.

'But there's more welcome in it than the sound of the words. There's elaichi, lemon grass, ginger and who knows what else, brewed with milk and sugar till every bit of flavour is leached out of the tea leaves and the spices. It's ambrosial.'

'Then why cut the pleasure in half?'

'So that you can quadruple it without guilt. And if your pocket is light, the brew's strong enough to last on your tongue till it acquires more weight.'

'Will you tell me your story tomorrow?'

'So, I'm coming tomorrow? You don't want to be left alone?'

'No. I don't.'

Avinash comes with a small wooden box. It has brass corners, studs and a drop latch. A mini chest in fact. He places it on a stool and removes from it a series of objects which he arranges carefully on the centre table. I notice that the table is dusty. I am ashamed. I have recently told my caretaker I don't need her. I rush to the kitchen to fetch a dusting cloth. I dust the table lifting each object to dust under it. In the centre is a photograph. He points to it.

'That's her. Sunetra. She once said, how did they know whether my eyes were going to be pretty or ugly or what? People shouldn't call babies by names they might not live up to. She lived up to hers. Look at those eyes. Even in a bad photograph they look at you with all the vivacity and vigour of life.'

He is silent. So am I. I look at the photograph from a distance. I do not wish to touch it.

'And this is the gajra she was wearing. She loved to deck her hair with flowers. I wooed her with flowers.' He points to a string of faded mogra.

'And this is our life together.' He picks up a small leather-bound album from the table and walks over to my side. He pulls up a chair beside me and begins to flip the pages of the album, the steady warmth of his breath on my neck. 'We were in the same class. We were thirteen when we fell in love.'

There are pictures of a school picnic, a class photo with everybody standing stiffly beside an even stiffer class teacher. There's one of a Diwali party with Avinash in churidar kurta and Sunetra in a sari. The last is a group photograph of young men in trousers and wispy moustaches and girls with burgeoning breasts. A banner at the back reads 'Farewell Class of '96'.

'We had to wait six years to marry,' Avinash says, returning to his seat. Pointing to a tightly bound stack of envelopes, he says, 'The letters we wrote to each other when I was in the States doing my Masters and she was here doing her MA in psychology. We loved pen-and-ink. I am happy we did. Our life during those years of separation is all there in black-and-white.'

He picks up a plastic bag. He extracts from it a ball of lemon-coloured wool with two small needles stuck in it. Hanging from one of the needles is an almost complete baby bootee. Most of the stitches have been cast off. Another hour of knitting and it would have been ready for ironing and stitching.

Avinash draws out its pair from the plastic bag and holds it up. He says nothing.

He picks up the last object from the table and hands it to me. It is a phone. 'That has the remaining two years of our life together. It's her phone. She loved recording every minute that we spent together. Towards the end you will see the picture I took of her in her fifth month. She turned her profile to the camera, pressed her kameez under her stomach to show off our little Bapudi, as she called the baby. Bapudi had just begun to kick. "Come, come, feel him," she would say giggling. "Her, not him," I would say and feel the little rippling movement under the skin of her belly. The beginning of life. Extinguished with her.

'What hurt most is that she was unrecognisable when I saw her. Her face was swollen, misshapen, discoloured. This was some other being wearing her clothes. They had brought her to this public hospital. Who? I don't know. Who had touched her last? Why weren't they attending on her? Get the doctor, I screamed. I think I kept screaming get the doctor. Strangers were milling around like people in a nightmare. She was lying alone on a high bed. I was screaming.

'I passed out.

'Her brother came. Her mother came. Her uncles. People who had disapproved of our marriage. We were the same age. That wasn't how it should be. We belonged to different castes. That wasn't how it should be. They had come to the wedding. Her side and my side. Both stood at a distance from us, from each other. They did the minimum required of families. Then left us to ourselves. We didn't care. We were world enough for one another.

That's how it happened.'

His voice has been flat through the story.

'How long ago?'

'Ten years. We had waited twelve years to marry. We were twenty-five.'

'What hit her?'

'A local.'

'She was crossing the tracks?'

'To get to me faster. She had been confirmed in her job after two years of internship.'

'And you went to the Sea Link?'

'Not consciously. Just drifted there after the families had departed. Families leave you to it. You'll get over it.'

'They do. So, you went to the Sea Link?'

'And leaned over the railing as you did.'

'Who spoke in your ear?'

'There was no time to speak. He did what he had to do. The cabbie who had dropped me and driven on. He reversed. He remembered how a cabbie had dropped someone on the link and the man had jumped off. He rushed over as I leapt. Grabbed my leg. I swung from his hands, kicking with my free leg. But there's only that much strength left in us when we have sorrowed and brooded and lost ourselves to despair. She was destined to die. I was destined to live. Not destined by anybody's plan. Destined by the randomness of life. It takes some away. Leaves some behind. The cabbie wasn't one of those hefty fellows. No mass. No muscle. But he had will. He led me into his cab, sat me down beside him, kept one eye on me and one on the road. He stopped at an Irani cafe on the main road and called for two cutting chai.'

'You survived without help?'

'The cabbie called me every day. "Theek ho na, saab?" he would ask. Then tell me where he was, describe the passenger he had just dropped. He was a fantastic raconteur, full of witty observations. Then suddenly he stopped calling. I was worried. I called his number. There was no answer. For days there was no answer. A colleague at work, a man as close to me as I would let man or woman be, said, "You had begun to look a little better. Like the man Sunetra had loved. You have become dour again."'

'I was surprised. We don't see ourselves as others see us. Nor was I interested any more in what I looked like. But I blurted out, "There's this cabbie. He hasn't called." The remark was so beyond my colleague's understanding that he felt it best not to go into what I meant. I saw the confusion on his face and let it be.

'One day the cabbie called. I was very angry with him. I shouted at him. "Where have you been? Do you know how worried I was? I tried calling you again and again. Why had you switched off your phone?"

'He said: "Saab, my phone was stolen. The bastard must have changed the SIM immediately. My family couldn't get through to me. Everybody was worried. I bought a new one today. My first call was to Ammi. My second is to you".'

'What was I to this man from eastern UP? This Muslim who had once said to me it doesn't matter if you believe in God or not. He doesn't need you. He is He with or without you. But you can always turn to Him when you need Him.

'I saw myself then. I looked small. Very very small.

'You can never tell what will turn your heart and mind away from gloom towards light. I don't know why it happened to me after those ten days of worrying. Perhaps I do, but I'm not going to try and put it in words.

'That's my story. I have healed. Sunetra lives in me. I talk to her every day. I tell her about every change that happens in the world which she isn't here to see. And there's something I share with her on her birthday and mine. I watch *Meghe Dhaka Tara*. Have you seen the film?'

'No.'

'We loved films. We'd sit together after dinner and watch a film. Hindi, Tamil, Marathi, Polish, American, Bengali—it's a world out there. This one was Bengali. It was my birthday. We had gone out for dinner. A seafood place. She loved seafood. We came home and watched this film. Imagine how these things happen. Why this film and no other? Our deal was she would pick a film on her birthday and I would pick one on mine. But since birthdays were celebrations, the film had to be bright, not dark. I thought I had picked *Closely Observed Trains,* a Czech comedy. I drew the DVD out of its cover and slipped it into the player. It turned out to be *Meghe Dhaka Tara*. I had mixed the DVDs up during the monthly defungus-ing.'

'"Not that one," she said. "But I'm okay with it if you are."

'"I'm okay with it only because I'm too lazy to get up and change it," I said.

'"I'll change it. It's your birthday," she said.

'"No. I don't want you to get up," I said. "It's my birthday."

'We laughed and watched the film. It was one of our favourites. Yet, however often we had watched it, we discovered something new each time. Sunetra wept in the end when the young woman cried, "*Dada aami baanchtey chai*" Dada, I want to live.'

Avinash's throat catches. He rises hastily, turning to

pick up his little chest of memories. With his back to me, he says, 'I'll see you tomorrow.'

He doesn't ask if I want to be alone.

❧

I have set up everything carefully for the evening. There is a huge hollow in my stomach. I don't want to do this. Can I not just be?

I must do this. What does it mean to just be?

Just being is not a human state.

If I am to be I will have to *be*. Not just be.

I set up a flask of hot tea with two cups and saucers. I bring out my tin box, the equivalent of Avinash's mini-chest and place it on the stool. I also set down a box of tissues beside it. The tears are swirling around in my stomach. They will come out.

'He was ten. He was diagnosed with acute lymphoblastic leukemia. I don't want to relive the horrors of his therapy. I only want to say that suddenly he became wise beyond his years. He talked about his grandparents a lot. They died within a year of each other when he was eight. He had seen death at close quarters. He had asked us many questions about death. He spoke of it now as though it was a common visitor to the house.

'During one of his stints in hospital he said "Mamma, can you bring me Ajji's Shaligram?"

'He used to sit beside his grandmother every Sunday during her puja. She told him many stories about the gods and goddesses whose idols and framed pictures she worshipped. He asked her one day what the round stone she worshipped was. Surely that wasn't a god. She told him it was Vishnu cursed by Vrinda to become a stone. Later she told him the story of Vishnu's betrayal of Vrinda. He listened to her, shocked. How could a god be so deceitful? How could he betray his most ardent devotee? How could she, a human, curse a god to become a stone? He shot these questions at his grandmother. She laughed and said, gods are gods but sometimes humans become powerful enough to curse them. Our ancient rishis understood these mysteries. They have left these stories for us to learn from. We must listen to them and believe in them.

'Aniruddha was angry. How can you just believe? So he asked his grandfather about the smooth round stone.'

'That was his name? Aniruddha?'

'Yes. I had to fight for it. Kishor's mother wanted him to be given one of Ganpati's names. She suggested Ameya. I wanted Aniruddha, the one who cannot be stopped. The one who will pour his heart and soul into all he does and not let any hurdle stand in the way.' I pause. 'Then death came and stood in his way.'

Avinash says, 'Sorry. I shouldn't have interrupted you.'

I pour myself a cup of tea and one for him.

'What did Aniruddha's grandfather tell him?'

'I was there, as curious as Ani. Dada told us a different story. He said millions of years ago, much of what we see as land today was sea. Then two land masses moved gradually towards each other. Their collision threw up the Himalayas. Shell creatures called ammonites which had been living in the sea, were now trapped in layers of rock. Gradually they turned into fossils. An ancient river flowed through deep gorges in the mountains. Many fossils got dislodged from the rocks and fell into the river. They lay on the river bed for centuries. One of them is your stone. The ribbed coil is the fossilised sea creature. Science is a slow process of discovery, Ani. When you grow up, you will read books about scientific discoveries that will amaze you…'

A sob rises to my throat. Avinash moves to my side and takes my hand in his. I shake my head. He looks at my face. I wipe my eyes on the sleeve of my kameez. I straighten up. He lets go of my hand and moves back to his place.

'I have told you this story because of what happened during Ani's last days in hospital. Once in a while, he would ask for his Shaligram. I would draw it out from under his pillow and hand it to him. He would spend a long time turning it over in his hand, feeling its smoothness and staring at its markings. He would return it to me saying, "Keep it Mamma" and close his eyes. I have no idea what seeing it and touching it meant to him. He was too young to articulate how he felt. Did he vaguely sense how transitory the here and now was in the context of the millions of years ago when living sea creatures had turned into fossils? Anyway, Dada. Dada said, "In ancient days, before scientists made their discoveries, people who picked up these fossils, didn't know about ammonites. They wondered at the unique coiled shapes that looked organic but were in fact stones. What did ancient human beings do when they saw something which they could not explain?"

'Dada paused and looked at Ani with a quizzical smile. "Don't know," Ani shook his head.

'"Simple. They made up stories. In those days everything mysterious and marvellous was taken as a sign of God. When it thundered, it was Indra doing his work. When it rained it was Varuna doing his. But what could they say about a stone in a river basin? The markings on the stone prompted the story. Doesn't this sign on your stone look like Vishnu's discus, and this like his mace, and this like his conch shell and this like his lotus? Well then, this is Vishnu. How did he become a stone? Somebody must have cursed him. Who could it have been? And why? Every question prompted our ancient storytellers to discover answers in their imagination. That is how the story of Vrinda and Vishnu was born. Isn't that the story Ajji told you?"

'Ani nodded, but looked worried. "She didn't tell it

like a story. She told it like it really happened."

'"Ani, in our religion we see God in everything. When you grow up you will wonder about God and His different names and the different stories about his birth and the different religions that men have created to worship Him. One day you will decide for yourself what is fiction and what is fact. Perhaps," and here Dada looked thoughtful, "you will decide that fiction is as true as fact."

'Ani looked puzzled and sighed. "I don't get it, Dada. But you will say I will get it when I grow up. Every question I ask ends like that. You will know when you grow up. When will I grow up, Mamma?"'

I swallow the sob in my throat and hurry to finish my story.

'You know the answer to his question. He didn't grow up. I went into a deep depression. Somewhere in the dark that enveloped me, I heard Kishor say, "I am leaving, Urmila. This isn't working for me. You are pulling me down with you. I don't want to go down. I want to live in the sun."

'He had found his sun. My sister, Saguna, who had come to stay with me, to be my moral support during Ani's last days. The woman who had remained single to look after my old parents, but free now that they were gone. Older than Kishor. Caring. That's the woman he had always looked for. I was a mistake. He needed a mother. Saguna needed a son.

'They left. I had lost son, husband, sister all in one stroke. Why not go myself? The Sea Link.'

Avinash and I have exhausted ourselves. We need time away from each other, with ourselves. One day he calls. He is tentative.

'How are you?'

'Okay, I guess. Back to work.'

'That's good.'

'I'm glad I chose work I could do from home. It was for Ani's sake. But it's good for me now. I don't have to face people.'

'You don't like people?'

'It's not so simple.'

'True. It isn't.'

There is nothing more to say. But I don't want the conversation to end.

'You said you would show me *Meghe Dhaka Tara*.'

'Yes, I did.'

'When?'

'Are you ready for it? It is a dark film. Tragic.'

'Let me give it a try. If I can't take it, we can always stop.'

'Do you have a player? I could bring mine across.'

'I don't. Couldn't we...'

There is a long pause.

'I'm not sure. It's just that...'

'Whenever. No hurry. I'm fine. Don't worry.'

He calls the next day.

'I'll pick you up in the evening, shall I? Our usual time?'

'I'll be ready.'

The film is dark. It is black and white. The heroine is a life force. Strong. Giving. Then all is taken away. That call at the end is all that is left of her, echoing in the hills, through trees, down into the river gorge, up into the sky. '*Dada aami baanchtey chai*'. I tremble. Avinash puts his arm around my shoulder. We sit like that, in silence, Nita's voice still echoing in the room, in our minds and hearts.

I have stayed the course. There are tragedies in life, tragedies we cannot even imagine. Lives we know nothing about. The future is a mystery. All we have is this moment. The life of this moment. The warmth of this moment. I sigh. I force myself to relax, muscle by muscle. My shoulders lose their stiffness. My jaw loses its tension. I rest my head against Avinash's shoulder. He leans his head on mine.

We decide to take Ani's Shaligram back to its original home. It gives Avinash reason to take leave. He has not taken any since Sunetra passed away. Sunetra will go with us and so will Ani. They will always be with us in their imperishable youth even as we grow older. They have become part of the unending sweep of time before us. March or September, the beginning of the two best seasons in Shaligram country—the Kali Gandaki river in Nepal. One of the oldest in the world, rushing through one of the deepest gorges in the world between the twin peaks of Dhaulagiri and Annapurna.

'March,' Avinash says decisively. 'Students will be busy studying for their exams. Achiever parents will stay up with them, anxious and sleepless. We will meet only elderly pilgrims on their way to Muktinath.'

We are in Pokhara waiting for our flight to Jomson. We look at the tiny plane, then at one another and laugh. We have both looked death in the face. If it comes to us in the Himalayas, crashing into snow in an unreliable plane, so be it. The plane feels steady enough when it takes off. Looking out, we see craggy mountain ridges just outside our window.

'Not very welcoming,' remarks Avinash, still considering them as a probable resting place. 'And there she is, the Kali Gandaki.'

We look down. The mid-morning sun glints off a shimmering ribbon of rippling grey mercury, cutting its way through inhospitable crags.

It is not a long flight. Our descent is rough and so is our landing on the wind-buffeted airstrip of Jomson. Around us the landscape is brown, wild, devoid of vegetation and human life.

We have decided to trek to Kagbeni where we hope to be within reach of the river basin. We will not go to Muktinath. The temple is for release from life into death. We are looking for release from death into life. The Gandaki will give us that.

It is spring. The rhododendrons are out in full bloom. Their colours look unreal against the clay-grey of the sheer striated rock faces that rise beside the narrow path we take. The rock faces themselves look unreal against the snow-capped Annapurna massif that rises beyond, serene and, to most humans, unassailable.

It is late afternoon when we reach Kagbeni. There is an awkward moment at the reception desk of the tiny hotel. The man at the counter gives us the key to a single room. Avinash does not look at me. I do not look at him. But at one and the same time, both of us say, 'Two rooms please.'

The next morning, we leave for Kagbeni. It is a long and dusty trail.

'Is this what you expected?' I ask.

'Not quite.'

'More green? Less grey?'

'H'm. But these crags tell us fascinating stories like wrinkles on old people's faces. When you look at them you believe, don't you, that they were thrown up millions of years ago when an earth-heaving movement occurred in the womb of the earth? A clash of plates. One riding up over the other. And, at the end of it, the sea vanished. These mountains appeared.'

We look for a way to descend to the river basin which appears rocky and dry from the trail.

'They said there's a footbridge across the river. We are to look for that.'

We almost miss it, it is so far down. We take the path that descends to it and we are there, standing on the rocks left bare by a river that has shrunk but will be in spate when the rains come and the snow at its mouth melts.

We are silent. Time, growth, erosion, being and not being, life and death, the eternal cycle...you see it written in the wide riverbed, the windswept heights around us. Only when I let my breath out, do I know I have been holding it.

This is the time. This is the moment. This the place where we hope to accept death.

'If the accident had left her a last breath, she would have used it to say, "I want to live." But perhaps, unlike Nita, she would have repeated many more times, "I will live. I will live." You would have loved her.' Avinash nods at me.

I slip my hand into his. 'We are here to offer Ani's Shaligram back to the river. But I don't want to do it...'

'Then don't. It's alright not to do what we came to do.'

'It's not that I don't want to. I do. But not just like that. I don't want to put it down here amidst the rocks, turn my back and go away.'

I realise I am looking for a ritual. A performance. Some act that will mark this moment, make it significant.

'Let us go down to the water,' Avinash says.

The rocks and boulders are uneven. We hold each other's hands and move forward slowly over them. We are at the water's edge. It is a narrow stream. But the gradient gives it motion. It flows fast. It will meet the Ganga. The Ganga will meet the sea. The Shaligram will not travel. It will lie on the riverbed, constantly washed by this water, fresh from melting snows, pure as the child who held it to himself as he gave himself up to Time.

Even as I bend to place the Shaligram in the running river, the skies open up in a cloudburst. I stand up, drenched. Avinash too is drenched. It does not rain in March. But sometimes things happen in nature that nobody expects. Nothing is stable. Everything is in perpetual motion. Resist while you can. Submit when you must.

We stand there, under the sudden shower, in a ritual of acceptance.

Silences

Basant, tall, floppy-haired, square-jawed, celebrated his eighteenth birthday yesterday. This morning his father Sharad, aged fifty-three, was admitted to hospital. Basant and his mother Girija aged forty-eight, the first hint of grey showing in her thick raven hair, rushed from Pune to be with him.

The hospital stands in a leafy district in central Mumbai. It is a municipal hospital with a national reputation. The poor come to it in droves. A worm's eye view of the corridors yields a crush of feet, shod, slipshod, unshod. The hospital is for the toilers of the earth, the workers, at looms and machines, courier boys, gig workers, security guards and suchlike. But there is a special room for patients who can pay for air-conditioning and a daily change of bed linen. That is the room Leela, aged fifty-eight, has requested for her brother.

The hospital where millions have breathed their last, is built in enduring stone.

It is Sharad's second day in hospital. He is lying on his side, gazing steadily at Girija. Girija sits on the unoccupied bed in the twin sharing room, gazing steadily out of the window at an old banyan tree. The aerial roots of the tree hang like the dreadlocks of an ancient sage. A man squats under it selling roasted gram. Beyond is a barber who has found shade under two massive aerial roots for his hair-cutting and shaving set-up. The set-up consists of a red plastic chair and a mirror nailed into a root. Basant sits beside Girija watching a line of ants on the floor scurrying purposefully to some place under the bed. He wants to see the place but does not want to disturb the fixedness of the scene by getting up and bending to follow the trail.

Leela Atya sits at the foot of Sharad's bed while Sharad's chawl neighbour, Nana Bobade, aged forty, recounts the happenings of the previous morning.

'I was downstairs getting my scooter started. It's old. Requires more warming up. Kicking and kicking. Just got it fired up when I heard a loud scream. My wife's voice. I ran upstairs and what do I see? Sharadbhau lying across our threshold, half in half out. What happened, I ask my missus. No use asking that one anything. She's too busy screaming. I have to think fast. Sharadbhau must be rushed to hospital. Other neighbours have left for work. Ambulance? It'll take hours to come. It will blow its siren. Nobody will move to let it go. Scooter is better. Then Sharadbhau sits up. Wants to go back to his room. Says he's all right. I say nothing doing. I'm taking you pillion to hospital. I tie him to me with a rope. That's how I get him here. He isn't saying anything now. But he told the doctor what happened. He called it a shooting pain. It started here, above my appendix, he said. Then went diagonally across my chest like this, up to my shoulder, here. He walked to our room and called my missus, he said. Then he didn't know what happened. Just thought I should come see how he is. Looks okay now, doesn't he? I'll be off then. Tell me if you need anything.'

Leela Atya nods. Bobade throws a glance at Girija who has been listening attentively. 'Lucky you were still there. Thank you for all the trouble you took,' she says quietly. Bobade smiles and leaves.

Girija's eyes return to the banyan tree. Leela Atya's gaze shifts from the departing man to her brother. Basant's eyes turn to the door through which the man left and Leela Atya's husband Ganesh Kaka is entering. Ganesh Kaka retired two years ago from his corporate job, but is into his second innings as a financial consultant.

Ganesh Kaka is a man of few words. Few hairs too. Whatever there is, hangs at the back in a fringe. That used to depress him till lately. But he has found a doctor now. Not a doctor really though he calls himself that. He's a man from Kerala. As a man from Kerala, he is assumed to have all kinds of ancient arts like oil massage and Kudiyattam running naturally in his blood. This person has concocted a magic oil. Simply rub it into your pate at night, wake up in the morning and find new hairs where there were none. The doctor is second generation Maharashtrian. He knows the local language well. He uses a Marathi proverb to put heart into his patients. *Thembe thembe tale saache*. A pond collects drop by drop. Single hairs soon make a thatch. You might not notice the growth but you must trust it is happening. Life is built on trust.

Leela Atya has been bolstering that trust each morning. When Ganesh Kaka wakes up and walks into the kitchen for his morning cuppa, she asks him to turn around. 'Oh yes!' she says gazing at the back of his head. 'I can definitely see new hairs.' Her husband cannot see the back of his head. But he trusts his wife. Life is built on trust.

Ganesh Kaka is one of those men who expect their office to collapse if they are a few minutes late. While he worked for ABC Capsules, he did not take a single day's leave. Sundays were leave enough, he said. He follows the clock to a split second even now in his second innings. As he steps into the room, he looks at his wristwatch. Then distastefully at Girija. Basant has risen from the bed to touch his feet.

'How does Pune suit your mother?' There is a sneer in Ganesh Kaka's voice which Basant ignores.

'Very well.'

'And you?'

'I don't mind it.'

'But you'd prefer to be here.'

Basant says nothing.

It is late evening. Basant is thrilled to be back in their one-storey chawl in Parel, one of the few of its kind still standing. His father's bed stands against the wall. He has made himself a little toilet block in the corner. The common toilet was never for him. He would go early to college to use the bathroom.

Basant looks around, breathes in the air. It still carries a faint aroma of his grandmother's cooking. When his grandfather lost his mill job, she started a mess. The mess became famous for its bangda fry, kulith usal and kombdi vade. When she found she couldn't accommodate her growing clientele in their single room, she bought a room on the ground floor and set up a proper mess there.

The last sitting in the mess ended at nine o'clock. The floor was swept and swabbed, the benches and chairs stacked against the walls and the room became Sharad and Girija's bedroom. There were no beds. They slept on floor mattresses, rolled up and carried upstairs in the morning. After Granny died Baba and Aai moved upstairs and Bandu began running the mess. At night the mess becomes his bedroom.

Bandu, fifty-six, soulful-eyed, thick-haired, silent, was twelve when he came from grandfather's village to stay with them. He was Grandpa Kashinath's nephew. He had failed his seventh standard board examination and his father had said go to Kashinath in Mumbai. He'll find you work. Kashinath found him a temporary job in a mill. After Kashinath had a stroke, his good friends found Bandu a series of temporary jobs in mills. A couple of years after Kashinath died and Bhagirathi bought the place downstairs for the mess, Bandu started working for her. Those days he slept in the common verandah upstairs.

Bandu has kept Sharad's room clean. The cousins exchange very few words beyond the practical. Sharad looks upon Bandu, first cousin though he is, as a poor dependent from the village. Bandu feels a sense of responsibility towards Sharad, now alone.

'I was downstairs, preparing for the lunch sitting,' he says to Girija, his eyes lowered. 'So much traffic. And the clatter of pots and plates. I heard Kaki scream. Must be a cockroach I thought. Then a mess member said Bobade has taken your cousin to hospital. I am a sinner. It should have been me. I should have run to help him.'

'You run the mess. That's enough,' Girija says soothingly.

'How is he?'

'Not too well.'

'Who is with him now?'

'Leela Atya. She'll do nights. We'll do days. Don't worry. You carry on with the mess.'

'Yes, if you don't mind. I must get up early for the market.'

'I'll come with you, Bhau.' Basant is excited.

'At 4 o'clock?'

'Yes. I'll set the alarm. Don't go without me.'

Basant is back home.

❧

The doctors have put Sharad through preliminary tests. The reports are clear. Sharad's heart, the first area of concern, is in more or less perfect order. It is the only organ about which Sharad shows concern.

'It's fine,' says the doctor. 'Ticking away like a young man's,' he adds, to relieve the patient's gloom.

'It is broken,' Sharad says, glancing at Girija. The doctor smiles neutrally and walks away, followed by his retinue of nurse and students.

Girija looks at the air above Sharad's head. Then lowers her eyes and looks straight at him. He cannot bear the impersonal sympathy in her eyes. He shifts his gaze to the ceiling. Basant glances from one to the other. He feels a familiar churn in his stomach.

'I have a friend named Socrates in Pune,' he says to his father, to lighten the atmosphere. 'Have you ever heard of someone called that before?'

'I hadn't even heard of someone called Basant before.' Sharad's eyes return to Girija. 'Your mother's choice. Because you were a spring child. Why not Vasant then? Because the raag is called Basant. Where's the connection between a raag and a child?'

'Sasubai saw the connection,' Girija says quietly.

'And the father didn't matter!'

❧

Five days down. Blood has been taken again. More X-rays and PET scans done. Sharad's lungs, arteries, veins, diaphragm, colon, liver, pancreas, gall bladder and kidneys have all been examined and found to be in working order.

The doctors are stumped. When doctors are stumped, they call for more tests.

Those reports too come back clear. Everything is as it should be. Nothing misplaced. Nothing swollen. Nothing oozing. Nothing tangled.

Basant sees it as a hopeful sign. But when Leela Attya comes at night and asks, 'What do they say?' and Girija answers in two words, 'Nothing wrong', she looks mournful. She calls Ganesh Kaka. 'All clear.' Before she can add another word, the line is cut. She puts her phone away and says to the air, 'All clear. Then what is wrong? Something has to be wrong.'

❧

Eight days on, Basant looks at his father lying wordlessly on his bed, visibly diminished. Eyes sunk. Voice grown fainter.

'He is a sick man.' Leela Atya entering the room, looks down at her brother and turns to Basant. 'Your father is a sick man, whatever the tests say.' Then, after a long pause, 'If nothing is wrong with him, why are the doctors keeping him here?'

Behind that question lurks an anxiety. Even a municipal hospital, though subsidised, charges for its special room. Girija has already withdrawn a large chunk from Sharad's meagre savings to pay the bills. Leela Atya recalls how bitterly she had berated her brother for making Girija a joint account holder with him. The woman had abandoned him. Run away. Deserted him. And he was sharing his bank account with her.

'She has not run away. We decided she should go. The climate didn't suit her. You know that. She used to have fits.' Sharad had looked at Leela reproachfully.

'Born and brought up in Mumbai and she has fits. Humph!'

'Well, she did. Aai knew.'

'Aai! She loved her daughter-in-law more than her daughter. Constantly shielding her. Did she recommend a joint account?'

'You know she was gone when I did it. It was my decision. I must support my wife. How do I send money across each month? My wife and son have a right to my money. When Basant is eighteen, I will transfer it all to his name.'

'And what will you live off?'

'I'll keep enough to see me through. And there's the mess. Anyway, we Jagtaps don't live long. Baba went at forty-two, Aai at sixty-six. I might not be around when Basant is eighteen. Even if I am, I'll be fine. Bandu is good with the mess though the competition gets harder every day. He still manages to give me a neat amount every month. He's honest.'

'But is your wife honest?' She put a special emphasis on 'wife'. Behind the question lay years of rage. The woman was a Brahmin, the one caste you could not trust. Why had Aai allowed this most objectionable of marriages to happen? The daughter of an advocate marrying a mill worker's son? Why had Girija's parents not objected to what was surely an even more objectionable marriage for them? Literally a climb-down. A chemistry lab romance! As unstable as chemicals that go up in smoke. But indulgent parents. Result? Woman runs off to live by herself. By herself? Who knows.

The conversation had ended.

Whether Leela Atya believes it or not, Girija has been honest. Sharad's bank book shows a modest sum of money withdrawn every month. The procedure since his hospitalisation has been for Girija to pay Ganesh Kaka by cheque and for Ganesh Kaka to pay cash to the hospital. This so that Sharad can keep a check on the outgoings. Sharad's account is not a cornucopia. After all, how much can a demonstrator in a private science college save in twenty-five years of non-pensionable service? Once the account is emptied, Ganesh Kaka will have to step in. Already he says every morning, 'I'm a retired man.' Leela Atya is not looking forward to what is coming.

It is Sunday. Sharad has been in hospital for ten days. Leela Atya has arrived earlier than usual, accompanied on this day by Ganesh Kaka who takes Sundays off. He wants to see 'personally what this is all about'. Leela Atya and Ganesh Kaka stand by Sharad's bed looking down at him. Basant stands near the window. Girija is where she always is, on the second bed which has remained unoccupied.

Sharad's eyes are closed. His skin is grey. There is a feeding tube in his nose because he has been refusing to eat. His thin arms rest immobile on the covering sheet. Leela Atya cannot believe that this man, her brother, once looked like Joy Mukherjee.

It is hot in the room. Ganesh Kaka is angry.

'Why is it so hot?'

'Something's wrong with the AC,' Basant says.

'I will not pay the full bill then.'

'I've already written the cheque,' Girija points out.

'We'll take him home today. You can see he is going. They are doing fuck-all for him. Just spinning money for themselves.'

Sharad's eyes open. He beckons Leela Atya with a feeble gesture. Ganesh Kaka stands between her and her brother. 'So how are you? We were just saying we'll take you home today. The doctors are doing fuck-all for you. You'll feel better at home. Girija and Basant are here to take care of you.'

Sharad's lips move. He gestures again towards Leela Atya. She steps forward and bends down to Sharad's moving lips.

'He says he wants to talk to Basant alone.'

Ganesh Kaka, Leela Atya and Girija leave the room. They stand in the crowded corridor outside the door.

The AC comes on with a bang and a whirr.

Basant moves to Sharad's bedside. He is afraid. He doesn't want to be alone with Sharad. He holds his breath. He does not know why. Sharad turns his lustreless eyes up to look at his son. He gestures to him to sit. Basant sits gingerly on the edge of the bed. Sharad pulls the feeding tube out of his nose. Basant is appalled. Sharad crooks his finger. Basant hesitates to bend. Sharad's hand grips his forearm and pulls him down. The hand feels like the claw of a predatory bird. Basant's ear is near Sharad's lips. Words dribble out weakly between them while the claw keeps its hold on his arm. 'I am going, son. You are eighteen. All the money in my account is yours. But I want you to do something for me. Ask your mother why she left me. Ask her. Tell her I loved her more than any man could love a woman.'

'You said Aai used to have fits, Baba,' Basant cannot help saying.

But Sharad's eyes have closed. Something subtle has happened to his face as though an unseen hand has passed over it. Basant has heard stories of people sensing their death moments before it comes. A famous actor once said, 'The comedy is over', laughed and died. His friend Manav's grandfather said, 'Chalo. I'm off,' and died. Has his father gone? How does one know? People feel the pulse, put their ear to the heart, hold a piece of cotton thread to the nose. Basant does none of these. He sits frozen. Then panicking, he rushes to the door. Stops. Gathers his wits. Walks through it. Leela Atya and Ganesh Kaka stand together on one side. Girija on the other.

'Well?'

'He said he's going.'

They rush in. Leela Atya feels Sharad's pulse, puts her ear to his heart, pulls a thread from her pallu and holds it to his nose. 'He's gone,' she whispers and bursts into sobs. Basant looks at Girija. Her face is turned away. She puts her handkerchief to her eyes. Ganesh Kaka's eyes are blank. Basant's dry.

This is the first death he has seen. The first time he

has been present in that moment when life ceases to be. He looks at Leela Atya. Her eyes are red and swollen. At Girija. Her eyes have not stopped streaming. He feels hollow. Why are his eyes dry? Is he not sad? He is filled with profound guilt. Horror.

❧

Basant is to perform his father's funeral rites. He does not know how. Ganesh Kaka says he will guide him. Basant's grandmother died when he was seven. Or was it eight? He had been playing carrom in the quadrangle downstairs when it happened. He was too young to attend the funeral. But he had been awed by the crowd that had gathered to accompany her on her last journey.

Today, only a handful of people sit in the small room. Leela Atya's in-laws, a couple of people from Sharad's college, Ganpat Dhaimode and Bhagwan Pawar—Grandpa Kashinath's friends—and Bandu, inconsolable. The mess is closed for the day.

'Your grandfather had a stroke,' Dhaimode says to Basant. 'We saw him collapse at the machine. We took him straight to the hospital. His right side became useless. He wept. We saw him weep again the day he lost his job. Twenty years we had worked shoulder to shoulder. He put his soul into that machine. But why should the owner care? Kashinath had become useless. Go. We don't need you. Friendships don't end like that.

We came here every day. This is where we sat. That is where he lay saying nothing. He had been a talker. The biggest of us three. But he turned silent. You could hear the silence in him. Two years and he was gone. Must have been his heart. His heart was broken. He loved that damned mill. He loved those damned machines, the noise, the going there, the coming back, the festivals, the singing, the plays. All gone. All, all over.' Dhaimode puts his shoulder cloth to his eyes. Pawar uses his sleeve. They weep for all that had been and now is not.

Dhaimode and Pawar walk behind Basant in the procession.

'Remember how good little Sharad was in the play we did for the inter-mill competition?' Dhaimode reminisces.

Pawar nods. '*Jugar*. Sharad should have won a prize.'

'With those tight-assed judges? For a play by a low-caste mill-worker who dared show Brahma rolling dice to decide who would be born as what?'

They fall silent. Then Pawar starts laughing noiselessly. 'Remember those vegetarian clerks who wanted Bhagirathi to serve them on a separate bench? "Away from these workers," they said.'

'Don't I? "Count yourself lucky I make your food in separate pots," Bhagirathi said. "Put your ass down next to theirs or go find your food elsewhere." What a lady!'

'That she was. Annapurna to all who came hungry to her door. But Kali to those who broke her rules.'

'One by one, the whole family is gone.' Dhaimode shakes his old head.

Ten days later, when Basant and Ganesh Kaka leave for Dádar beach with the pindi that will set Sharad's soul free of its earthly attachments, Leela Atya sighs, 'Poor Sharad. A lifetime of unfulfilled desires. Which crow in God's sky will touch his pindi?'

Several crows come. The first one gets the best pickings.

Basant is sunk in gloom. They have just returned to Pune. He still feels the weight of the funeral pot on his shoulder. He feels even more the weight of his father's question on his chest. Girija is putting their things away. Is she sad? He can't tell. How does sadness feel? Do different people feel sad differently?

'Shall I make you something to eat, Basant? You must be hungry.' Girija turns to her son whom she has always called by his full name. The vermillion mark on her forehead blazes. It is small, but bright red. It is supposed to be erased when a woman loses her husband. But many don't do it. If girls who are waiting to be married and spinsters who have lost or willingly given up the chance to marry wear it, why connect it with marriage? Basant is used to seeing that red dot between his mother's eyebrows. He cannot imagine her without it.

'No Aai. I'll last till dinner,' he says. He is surprised to hear his voice come out weak and trembling. Girija walks across to him and holds his head tight against her stomach. She bends her head. Lays her cheek against his hair. When she feels him pull away, she sits down beside him.

'I need to sing,' she says, searching his eyes to see if he is hurt. Basant feels a surge of relief. She needs to sing. She has rediscovered music in Pune. Found a guru who is an excellent teacher. She charges only autorickshaw fare from Deccan Gymkhana to their room and back. 'I got music free from my father. I am happy to give it free to a student who takes it with love and passion,' she said the first day she came. Music has become Girija's speech. She does not say much otherwise.

Girija takes her tanpura out of its flower-printed cover and lowers herself to the floor with it. Laying it across her lap like a baby, she begins to tune it. Her ear catches subtle notes that Basant's ears cannot. A line appears on her forehead as she twists the pegs of the instrument, tweaks the strings and, for the ultimate fine-tuning, moves a tiny thread on the bridge till she hears the perfectly pitched resonance of the drone notes. Holding the instrument close to her ear like a trusted confidante, she runs her fingers over the strings, filling the room with the eternal constancy of the drone notes. Once they fill her outer and inner ears so completely that no other sound exists, she slips her base note in to merge with them. She has not sung for twelve days. Her voice is dry. She clears her throat once, then again and makes a second attempt. Her voice responds. She moves smoothly into the initial explorations of the melody without rhythmic accompaniment. Then, very quietly, she introduces the first line of the composition, starting the metronome on the first beat of the line.

Basant picks up the book lying on a stool beside him and opens it at the page where he had hurriedly placed a scrap of paper when the phone call came from Mumbai. For an entire week before that, Socrates had not talked of anything else but this book. It had been a cult thing in his father's times. 'See if it makes any sense to you,' Prof Sawant had said when he handed over the much-used copy to his son. 'It's about a father and a son and a journey and values.' Socrates had zipped through it. Basant knew that if he was to have any conversation at all with his one and only friend in Pune in the following months, he would have to read *Zen and the Art of Motorcycle Maintenance*. The title juxtaposed entities from two diametrically opposite worlds. That intrigued Basant.

But he is finding it hard to concentrate on the page. The words are familiar symbols that make independent sense, but together they make no sense at all. Something else needs to be made sense of more urgently. He needs to make sense of the storm of emotions tossing around in his chest, in his stomach, in the hollows of his body. Is this sadness?

Girija is singing a composition that Basant knows. The raga and the words are filled with unease—the raga because it has an anchor note missing and the words because of what they say.

What did I do? Was I wrong? My heart is troubled.

Girija elaborates on the refrain, her voice coaxing every shade of meaning out of the words. Her voice expands when she moves into the main stanza.

I told you, but you would not understand. I too did not understand.

Basant puts his book down. There is no point in trying to read. Dusk is falling. The room has darkened. He does not want to get up to switch on the light. He sits with eyes closed till the song winds down.

You would not understand, you would not understand, you would not understand…

Girija sings the phrase three times, announcing the finale. The words and notes of the third iteration echo in the air before they die. A long, deep silence follows. Girija sits with bowed head, absolutely still, allowing the rhythm in her body to return to its prosaic pace. She pulls the cover of the tanpura towards her and zips the instrument in. She gets up heavily, cradling the tanpura in her arms and places it, stem up, in its corner. It is a gift from her teacher, the instrument her own daughter had used before she married into a family that said no music in our house, please.

Girija twists her torso left and right to loosen it. She switches on the light and turns to look at Basant. Her eyes are twin pools of intense concern. She sits down beside him, takes his hand in both of hers and says quietly, 'I am sorry your father is gone.' Then, almost inaudibly, 'He was…a good man.'

'Why did you leave him then?' This is the moment to ask her that. Basant's mouth forms the words but they do not emerge. Girija strokes his cheek, sits looking at him, then rises. The moment is lost. She begins to cook their dinner.

Girija is an inventive cook. Taste flows from her fingers as music flows from her throat. The cheapest leafy vegetables in the market turn into a melody of flavours in her hands.

❧

Pramila, Socrates's mother and Prof (Dr) Hrishikesh Sawant's wife is no cook. At snack time in the evening, the family, and Basant when he is there, eat vegetable puffs from the next-door bakery or pohe from an eatery further down the road. Pramila finds cooking tiresome.

'So would I,' Prof Sawant says in her defence.

A jolly woman called Indira Kaku cooks their evening meal. They are not foodies. They have chapatis, vegetables, dal and koshimbir every day. Most times, they don't even notice what they are eating. On the rare occasions that Indira Kaku cannot come, Pramila makes rice in the pressure cooker, and the family has it with curd and pickles.

Pramila and Hrishikesh met as students at Elphinstone College in Mumbai. Both went to Cambridge, she to do Mathematics, he to read Philosophy. They head their respective departments in Fergusson College now. When she returns from college she boils a mug of water in the micro, dips a sachet of tea in it and sits down to read. When he returns from college, she looks up from her book, they wave to each other, he boils a mug of water, dips a sachet of tea in it and sits down to read. When Socrates returns from college (he has chosen to go to the one which enjoys an age-old rivalry with theirs), he boils a mug of water, dips a sachet of tea in it and sits down to read. If Basant comes at snack time, as he often does, he too follows the tea routine. Although the family reads most evenings, there are times when it argues heatedly or simply chats.

Like the time Socrates said, 'Why did you name me Socrates? It ruined my life at school.'

Prof Sawant glanced at Pramila, laughed apologetically and said, 'I wanted to hold truth in my arms.' Pramila raised her eyebrows pointedly.

'Look. I was twenty-eight. An idealist.'

'The correct word is MCP.'

'That being…?' Socrates.

'Male Chauvinist Pig.'

Prof Sawant made a mock whipped dog face.

'Why did you allow it, Mom?'

'Our power equation was different then. I was raised to be a woman. He was raised to be a man.'

'The names she suggested were impossible.'

'Not Pythagoras, I hope.'

Prof Sawant chuckled. 'No, not quite that bad.'

'Sensible ones in fact,' Pramila sniffed. 'Dhananjay. Aaditya, Chetan, Manav…'

'Take your pick,' Prof Sawant said. 'You are eighteen. You have the right to change your name.'

'I want to be Anand.'

'Then be Anand. Do you want to change your name, Basant? You'll soon be eighteen.'

Basant laughed, shaking his head. And Socrates remained Socrates.

Basant enters without his book. He knows the family will close their books when they see him at the door. They will not drench him in sentiment over his loss. They will only want to know the what and the how of his father's death. He can speak to them about it. He can open his mind to them. He can ask them about the things that are weighing on his mind.

He answers their questions.

Age? He was fifty-three I think. I can't be sure. As

far as I know yes, he was healthy. We hadn't heard of any health problems. Yes, it was sudden. No, the doctors could not diagnose the problem. He couldn't keep any food in. He lost weight at a frightening rate. We would leave at night, come the next morning and see more bones than flesh. Yes, that's the word. He wasted away.

Then he asks a question.

'They asked me to carry a small clay pot on my shoulder and go round the body. It was filled with water but it had holes. Water streamed out as I walked. Then I had to throw the pot over my shoulder to break it. I couldn't bring myself to do it. I stood frozen. Ganesh Kaka kept urging me to throw it. Finally, he shouted at me. That made me angry. I threw the pot in anger. Nobody would tell me what the pot meant. Perhaps nobody knew. But I want to know. What was the pot all about?'

A silence ensues. Prof Sawant sighs, shifts forward in his chair and looks at Basant. Socrates is seated next to him. Both are alert.

'The pot…' Prof Sawant begins, '…symbolises two things. It is the human body and it is material attachments. The water dripping from the pot symbolises the dead person's soul leaving the body. The breaking of the pot and the water draining out tells the soul it has left the body. It must now leave behind all the body's attachments to material possessions…even to human beings.'

Dr Sawant stops speaking. A sob rises to Basant's throat. He tries to swallow it, but it won't stay down. Basant breaks down crying away all the pain and confusion of the last two weeks. Socrates fetches a glass of water and places it on the peg table beside him. Pramila brings a box of tissues from their bedroom.

'Sorry,' Basant says, rubbing vigorously at his eyes and nose with a tissue. He gulps down half the water in the glass.

'Feel better?' Pramila.

'Way better. But there's something else.' Basant waits to find the words. Then narrates simply what his father asked him to do before he died. 'I will have to ask Aai about it. I don't suppose Baba's hanging around up there waiting for me to ask. That would make me Hamlet.' He laughs nervously. The others laugh too. 'No, it's not for him. It's for me. I want to know. Why did we suddenly leave Mumbai after Granny died. All these years I had thought it was because Aai started getting fits in Mumbai. But that wasn't it.' Basant looks lost.

'Perhaps it really was because the climate in Mumbai didn't suit your mother,' Pramila suggests. 'It happens. Mumbai is humid. Bad for people with chest problems. Does she have asthma?'

'No, she doesn't. You should hear her sing. She has what they call a pahadi voice. I suspect the health problem was only a story to tell people. If it were true,

Baba wouldn't have used his last breath to ask why Aai had left him.'

Prof Sawant speaks. Normally he makes deep eye contact when he does. But now he stares at the floor as though what he is about to say is written there. 'There are silences in every family. It is like a pact. Nobody says in so many words that we will not speak of this. But they don't. The silence sets everybody free except the victim. Oh yes. There is always a victim. And a wrongdoer. The silence shields the wrongdoer and betrays the victim. Most times for family honour. Your grandfather went to jail. That can't be hidden. Why was he jailed? A silence prevails. The truth goes underground. Gossips will gossip but the family has not contributed to its own dishonour.

'And then there is the individual victim. Child abuse, incest, impotence, homosexuality, children born out of wedlock...If you don't speak of it, it's not there. But it is there in the victim's mind, destroying his life...'

Prof Sawant looks at Basant now. 'I hope it doesn't happen to you. But you might have to live with silence.' His voice has an edge.

Pramila has not taken her eyes off her husband. 'Tell him that circumstances play a major role in these things. Tell him there are things that a mother simply cannot tell her son. Tell him he must learn not to hold it against her. Tell him it is not easy to do. Tell him even grown-up men, men who have spent their entire adult lives with the world's greatest philosophers, have not quite managed to forgive their mothers.'

Prof Sawant leaves the room.

Girija's teacher is at the door, saying goodbye. Girija looks down the ill-lit street expecting to see Basant at the far end. He times his return from the Sawants to coincide with her teacher's departure. He is late. Girija turns away, leaving the door ajar. Moving to the narrow kitchen where only one human being of moderate size can work, she gets down to making dinner. She is worried about Basant. Something is weighing on his mind. Sharad must have said something upsetting to him on the last day. What was it? She dared not ask though she thinks she knows. But the silence covering what he said stands between her and Basant.

She is cleaning a banana flower. The process is sticky, but the result very tasty. Sharad wanted to sell off the chawl room in Mumbai and buy a place in Pune so we could be together again. I said no. Very brutally. There was no other way. Had he talked to Basant about that? If Basant brings it up with me, I will find it impossible to say a word. How can I tell him I did not want your father anywhere near me? He was...obsessed. Always touching, feeling, squeezing. At night...the memory of those nights brings up the puke in me. He did not do what my college friend had said he would. He played with me like a toy and kept mumbling, 'I love you, oh how I love you.' Then he went into the kitchen. When he came back, he put his hand on my breast and went to sleep. I wanted to menstruate every day to keep him off me. Menstruation days were my free days. Sasubai noticed that they came regularly every month. They kept coming for five years. The family said I was barren. The neighbours taunted me. Sasubai wondered.

She said, 'I'm taking you to a doctor. Nobody decides that a woman is barren. Only a doctor.'

I did not want to go to a doctor. Sasubai insisted. The gynaecologist examined me and told Sasubai what I did not want her to know. I was still a virgin.

Sasubai said, 'Talk to him. Tell him. He doesn't know. He is innocent.'

'What do I say? I don't know.'

'Tell him what your mother told you.'

'Aai told me nothing,' I said, holding back what my college friend had said.

'I will talk to him then,' she said. 'I want a grandchild.'

Sasubai was a determined woman. She had worked hard to put Sharad through school and college to save him from a mill job. Chawl rooms are not made for privacy. Although she whispered when she spoke to Sharad, her voice carried.

'A woman needs to have a baby. For her health.'

'I don't want her to have a baby,' Sharad said. 'It is painful. I don't want her to be in pain. I love her too much.'

'There is also the pleasure before the pain. Should she not have that?'

'Chhee. She is not like that. She is pure.'

I resigned myself to a lifetime of fondling, squeezing, slobbery kisses and childlessness.

One day Sasubai said, 'I have told Sharad you are not going downstairs today. I want you here.' After a pause she said, 'In the old days, kings who could not have heirs allowed their queens one night with a commoner. My son won't give you what is your right. I have made arrangements with a good, discreet man to do what needs to be done. He is under oath to me never to speak of it.'

I could not believe what she had just said. My shock must have been obvious.

'I will not force it upon you. Think about it. Remember families don't always grow by legitimate seeds. Not even royal families. You need not think you are doing something dishonourable. If you want a baby as much as I want a grandchild, this is the only way. Think about it.'

'I don't want a baby this way. I want a baby made with love,' I said.

'You've lost that chance girl,' she said brutally. 'Think about it.'

I wandered around like a lost spirit the whole of the following day. I had nobody to talk to. Even if I did have, I could not have talked about this.

Towards evening, I pulled myself together. I was thirty. Married. But still a virgin. Sharad was the handsomest man I had ever met. He loved me. I had dreamt every day of our lovemaking. Of sleeping in each other's arms. Of waking up in each other's arms. My body had craved his touch. Now his touch revolted me. Perhaps having a baby could be my way out. My body would change. He would hate what it might become.

I wanted a baby, whichever way it came. I had Sasubai's blessings for it. It could not be wrong.

'I want a baby,' I said to Sasubai.

On the fifth day of my next menstrual cycle, a man slipped into the room in the dark while Sasubai stepped out. I closed my eyes as Sasubai had instructed me to do. 'I don't want you to see him. He is a decent man. You are a decent woman.'

The man was extraordinarily gentle and respectful with my body. He was not practised. But we managed. And I am not ashamed to say, I found some pleasure in what happened.

Sasubai and I waited. It was now or never. The experiment could not be repeated. If it did not fructify, I would resign myself to a childless life.

Perhaps the man's seed was strong. Perhaps my ova were plentiful and waiting. Fertilisation took place and the creation of a human baby began its long and magical process in my body. I felt sad for Sharad. Did he wonder how this could have happened without his will, without his participation.

He did not ask. We did not tell.

My body gradually swelled to accommodate and feed the new life. Sharad stopped looking at me. He sulked. I was profoundly grateful for both. It allowed me to be with my baby in peace and joy. Sharad did not come to the hospital to fetch me home. Sasubai came with Bandu. And yet, when we came home, Sharad smiled lopsidedly and said, 'He's a Jagtap all right.' Having said that, he decided Basant was his son which gave him the right to argue over the baby's name.

'When will you come downstairs to sleep?' he asked one day. He kept his voice down. But of course, Sasubai must have heard.

'Never,' I said equally softly.

Sasubai must have heard that too.

'She's nursing. She must be with the baby now,' she told her son.

Basant was the delight of her life. He was with me only when I nursed him. At all other times he was hers. She took him to school and fetched him back. She made snacks every day for his lunch box. She left the mess more and more to Bandu's care. Basant became the sun around which she spun. If Sharad did not want to feel isolated, the only way was to participate in bringing up

Basant. He made an effort. He bought him little toys and later, books. He also stayed out late some evenings. Nobody asked him why.

When Sasubai had her heart attack, Basant was at school. A month after she died, I left Mumbai.

How do I tell Basant this story? How do I tell him that I don't know to this day who the man was who fathered him. I had faith in Sasubai. She must have chosen a good man, a trustworthy man, a healthy man. That was enough for me.

❧

Basant came back on silent feet. 'The door was ajar. Why?' He walked slowly to the kitchen corner.

'I'm making banana flower bhaji today. You like that.'

'Why have you never asked me what Baba said to me before he died?'

Girija's hands stopped cutting, the knife half-raised.

'Because I know.' She returned to her chopping.

'How can you know? You were not in the room.'

'I know because I knew your Baba.'

'So tell me. Why did you leave him? He said he…'

'Loved me?' Girija looked at her son. 'Do you know what he meant by that?'

Basant was angry. 'Don't ask me counter questions. I want an answer.'

Girija stopped chopping the banana flower and turned to face her son.

'Well, you cannot have an answer. There are things mothers can't tell their sons. This was between your father and me. He shouldn't have burdened you with our problem, particularly when he knew the answer. You must trust me when I say I left your father because I could not have lived with him for a moment longer.'

'I asked. She said what you said she would. There are things mothers can't tell their sons.'

'You look angry.' Pramila.

'I am. I'm not speaking to her.'

Prof Sawant let himself in and made straight for the kitchen. Coming out with his mug of tea, he asked, 'Where's yours, Basant?'

'Don't feel like tea.'

'Where's your friend?'

'Stayed back for practice.'

'Are you lying to us or did he lie to you? Sounds like a girl to me.'

Basant shrugged. 'Perhaps there are things sons don't tell their fathers.'

They laughed. Socrates entered as their laughter faded.

'What's the joke?'

'Some jokes that can't be repeated.' Pramila.

Socrates was annoyed. 'The joke seems to have been on me.'

'I just wanted to know from Basant if the practice you stayed back for was with a girl.'

'You have one-track minds. I was auditioning for a play.'

'Pramila used to do that kind of thing. She even landed a role once.'

'And your father sulked because I held the hero's hand.'

❧

'I'm going to Mumbai for a few days.'

They were seated at the folding table, having dinner. Girija had made spinach with peanuts and tamarind which Basant loved. He had forgotten that he was not talking to her. She made no comments on the change.

'When?'

'Tomorrow.'

'Suddenly?'

'Want to be there for a bit. It's home.'

'There's nobody there to make it home.'

'My friends are there. I didn't get time with them when Baba was ill.'

'You've grown up. They've grown up. It's never the same.'

'I'll find out. And there's Bandu Bhau. You aren't saying you don't want me to go, are you?'

'No, not at all. It's a way to figure out things. Chawl life isn't easy. Your grandmother taught me to deal with it.'

'Would you like to come?'

Girija looked at Basant carefully. Then said, without a trace of emotion, 'No. I hated it. But bring me back Granny's photograph. It's in her trunk. She was dressed up for Ganapati. Brinjal coloured sari with a broad jari border and her mother-in-law's nath in her nose.'

Basant entered the mess as the last member left. He had spent the day looking up friends. Girija was right. The old connection had snapped. The conversation was forced.

Bandu set down two thalis on a bench, one for Basant, one for himself. Basant sipped the sol kadhi first. It tasted exactly like Granny's.

'What brought you back again?'

'Everyone goes home in the long vacation.'

Bandu looked at him briefly, then down at his thali.

'How is Girija Vahini?'

'Fine. Sings. Cooks.'

'A good woman. She was like a mouse when I first came. Bhagirathi Kaki protected her. The chawl women sniggered, called her names because she couldn't have children.' There was a long pause. 'Then you came and they shut up.'

'I came late. There must have been a reason for that.'

'If there was, I don't know it. But your father was a good man.'

'Yes. Aai said that. What does it mean, good man? You said she was a good woman. Now you say he was a good man. Both good, so why could they not live together?'

'I don't know, Basant. But I can tell you what good means. It means you do not harm anyone knowingly.'

'But if you harm someone unknowingly? Are you still good?'

'I don't know. I don't know. I don't ask myself these questions. Dropped out of school, came here, worked in the mill, learned to cook and keep accounts. Listened to my elders. Respected every word and wish of Kaki's. That's all I know.'

'Was your father a good man?'

'He was, except…'

'Except?'

'Nothing. There were bad times. I want to forget them.'

'You haven't still?'

'Takes time. They're your father and mother. You don't want to blame either.'

'Why didn't you marry, Bandu Bhau?'

'No time. No money. How's the food?'

Basant looked at Bandu's shuttered face. A long silence later he sighed and said, 'Just like Granny's.'

❧

The corners of the room had grown dark, the shadows inching towards the centre. Girija switched on the light. Clouds had been gathering all evening. The wind, blowing in through the window in gusts, carried news of rain. Pune rain was lighter than Mumbai rain. But sometimes there were thunder showers. Tonight could be the first, wetting the cement of the city and the parched earth of the countryside. Girija turned from the window to see Basant standing in the doorway.

'Arre! You're back already? You said…'

'Yes. But I decided to come.'

'Did something happen? Did something upset you? Did someone say something? I knew…'

'Nothing Aai. Nothing happened. Nobody said anything.' Basant's voice had lost the edge it had acquired in the last three months.

'So then?'

'You were alone. I came.'

Basant swung his backpack off his shoulders, opened an outside pocket and drew out an envelope.

'Here.'

'What?'

'Granny.'

Girija sat down with the envelope and drew out the faded photograph. Basant sat beside her. They looked down at an elderly woman seated in a plastic chair dressed in a nine-yard sari, her thin hair tied back in a bun, a large round red mark on her forehead, no jewellery except for a mangalsutra, a pair of thin gold bangles and a nath, her expression self-consciously stiff.

Tears gathered in Girija's eyes and fell rapidly down her cheeks. Basant put his arm around her shoulders. As mother and son sat together, a gentle patter started outside.

Basant looked at the fine needles of rain that might soon turn into a roaring sheet of water.

'Will you sing, Aai?' he said. 'A fast composition.'

'Must think of one without saiyyan or balaman. Just about clouds, thunder, lightning, rain.'

She rose. There was a spring in her step as she walked to her tanpura. She settled down, the tanpura at her ear. Without any preliminaries, she plunged straight into the words: *Bijali chamake barase,* in raag Malhar, her voice rich and true.

Lightning flashes, clouds rain down/The thunder makes me fearful/ Clouds thunder, lightning flashes / Pihu pihu goes the cuckoo / Where shall I go, what shall I do/ My heart aches with thirst.

Basant picked up his book, turned to the interrupted page and began to read.

The Way Home

'Tomorrow I won't go to the clinic,' Shrikant said to Gulab.

'Saheb?'

'I'm retiring. I will stay home. Help you look after Usha.'

They were standing in the sit-out of the small house in the leafy Khar lane which Shrikant's municipal engineer father had built when he retired, using his Provident Fund and gratuity, on land that had belonged to the family since the eighteenth century. It was a neat ground-plus-one bungalow. Shrikant's father had built it small to spare land for a garden. Shrikant's mother had loved plants. She had returned indoors from watering them one morning when she had found her husband dead in his chair. She had died within a month of him, leaving Shrikant owner of its two bedrooms, hall, kitchen, pantry and sit-out. Built in stone, *Visava* had stood firm on its foundation through two generations and would continue to stand for a few more.

The day was windy. The small bushes in the garden stood steady against the gusts. But the two coconut trees in the corner swayed with a great swishing of fronds and the branches of the gulmohar, standing beside the path that led to the gate, tossed and dipped, their load of flowers that had blazed red through April and May, flying off, their vivid season coming to a dramatic end.

In better times, Usha had begun to tell Gulab the story of the gulmohar, got distracted into diversions down which she had ambled absently, losing the story till Gulab had prodded her gently back to it.

'When we were on our honeymoon—not to Kashmir or anything—only Matheran—Shrikant wanted to ride on the toy train…he was like a child…so innocent. My friend Prabha…she was my sister…we were five, Papa called all five of us by dawn names…He wanted a son…that was after me…Arun…my friend Arun went to Oxford…no Cambridge…somewhere…'

'Was that your brother?'

'No, no, no. Five sisters. They called us panchkanya… that means five…daughters…'

'So, who came after you?'

'I told you, Arunima. My father wanted a son…he had names for us all. Dawn names. He wanted Uday. I wonder where Uday is. My father's name was Uday. My mother's name was…'

'Did you have a brother called Uday?'

'No Gulab. We were five sisters. Panchkanya. Five daughters.'

'So, there was no Uday.'

'There was Udaya. Then came Dawn.'

Usha burst into laughter. Usha had laughed a lot in those days.

When Shrikant asked Gulab that night how the day had been and if Usha had talked, he completed the story of the five sisters for her. Prabha, the eldest, had been a brilliant cardiologist, never married and died of jaundice. Arunima, a chartered accountant had married a Bengali professor and lived in Delhi. Udaya, a mountaineer, had lost her husband in a landslide in the Garhwal Himalayas and had set up an NGO helping local women to bring their traditional weaves to the market. Dawn, the youngest, had married a Dutchman and lived in Amsterdam. Shrikant pulled out the children's atlas to show Gulab where that was.

'Prabha was my friend from medical school,' he said. 'That's how I met Usha. When we came home from our honeymoon in Ooty…'

'Not Matheran?'

'Ooty. We saw a sturdy little sapling sitting inside the fence with a note that said, "Wish you two a long and happy life together". It was unsigned. We still don't know who left it there.'

'Did you not go to Matheran for your honeymoon, saheb?'

'No Gulab. I said Ooty. Why do you ask?'

'Bai said you liked to go on the toy train.'

'She did?' He had thrown his head back and laughed. 'That's right. I loved the toy train as a boy.'

The following day Usha had greeted Gulab with a puzzled question. 'Who are you?'

'Bai, I'm Gulab. You like my hair, no? With the flowers? I've worn a mogra string today.'

She turned around. Her thick glossy black hair was done in a characteristic Koli bun, with the smooth swathe of the tail spread sideways over the knot and tucked in. When she turned back, the light had gone out of Usha's eyes.

A brisk, pre-monsoon shower had started now. Shrikant stood looking at the path. The paving stones, washed clean, glistened.

'She won't swallow, saheb,' Gulab said. She had been trying to spoon minute quantities of bread dipped in milk into Usha's mouth.

'She won't because she can't, Gulab. She can't. It's the last stage. Her muscles are giving way.'

This was the stage he had dreaded all along. The moment when he would have to say firmly to Senthil that he wasn't going to move Usha to hospital to be fed through a tube. Shrikant and Usha had discussed and decided this when she was diagnosed.

'I want to die here, Shrikant. In the natural way. We know this disease. We saw Jitish through it. A doctor.

And what happened? He died anyway. If the body is shutting down, we must let it go the way it wants.'

The shower ended as suddenly as it had begun. Shrikant stood looking down at Usha. 'Ush, I'm off darling. Try and eat a little if you can.'

She turned her eyes up in the direction of his voice. He bent down, ran his hands over her face, and kissed her forehead. Her face was blank.

Shrikant had plenty of time to think in the car. He didn't play music. He watched the small stone house in his rearview mirror till he turned the corner. Even after his parents' death, *Visava* exuded the happiness of their life. When people visited for the first time, they inevitably remarked, 'How serene it is here.'

Bhalchandra Uncle was the one who disrupted the serenity every time he visited from the Dadar lodge where he had lived all his life. He quarrelled with everything, from his brother's choice of newspapers to his sister-in-law's cooking. Every time some relative, close or remote, remarked on his rootless existence, he would explode, 'Rootless? I beg your pardon. The room in the lodge is my home. The clinic is my workplace. What is rootless about that? Why should I bother with a household when I have no wife and children?'

Uncle was the one who had driven Shrikant to do medicine. Which was just as well. His father was too mild a man to drive him to do anything. And Shrikant certainly had no plans of his own when he joined the science stream at college.

'Focus on Bio, not Maths,' Uncle had said in his scolding voice. 'Get into medical college. There's a clinic waiting for you. As soon as you get your degree, you move in and I move out. To Devrukh. To die in peace.'

He lived for many years in the family home in Devrukh after he retired, driving the caretaker crazy with his fastidiousness. But he died in peace as he had wished. He went to bed one day and did not wake up. Shrikant had always suspected that the gulmohar sapling was his gift.

Senthil, his medical college classmate and Shrikant had often talked of retiring. But then said it was wrong to retire while their wits and skills were still intact. 'And certainly not while Farokh Udwadia Sir is still going strong,' they said, shaking their heads in disbelief and admiration.

Shrikant hit a red light at St Michael Church. There was a long wait ahead. There would be one more change of lights before he got through. And then the slow crawl through the narrow ribbon of road left to traffic beside the fortifications of the everlasting work on the Metro.

Shrikant called Senthil.

'Got a minute?'

'Just about.'

'I'm retiring today.'

'Yes.' Senthil was a neurologist. He had looked after Usha and knew it was endgame for her.

'There's a question that's bothering me. Occasionally

Usha refers to our past. Like, "Have you had your ice cream?"'

'Ice cream? Why?'

'Well because…I used to eat a lot of it. Two scoops, three scoops at a time even.'

'Oh? Okay. Quietly at home I guess.'

'Like others drink, no?' Shrikant countered. 'Now, do you think a part of her brain could be activated if I talked to her about the past. You think she would respond?'

'You want a benign reply or a brutal one?'

'I don't want you to tell me the human brain is a mystery. I know that. But if you can give me hope based on cases you have treated…'

There was a long pause.

'What if I say there is indeed a chance that old memories might stir something in her?'

'Then I would talk to her about old times. I'm going to be at home with her all day. We never had that kind of time together when we were working. I'd be happy if I saw even a trace of a smile. If something I said cleared the fog in her brain for a moment and brought light into her eyes.'

'It is worth trying, Shri. Let us see what happens. Experiments like that don't require technology. Plain simple love. Who knows? Who knows?'

Shrikant walked into his clinic at the dot of ten as he had done for decades.

'Can you come in, Khambe?' he said to the compounder as he walked in. 'I won't be long,' he said to the two patients waiting for him.

'Sit down, Rajabhau.'

Khambe sat on the edge of the chair, adjusting his spectacles with a blend of self-importance and humility.

'I had told you last month that I would soon be retiring. You remember that, don't you?'

Khambe nodded.

'Well, today's my last day.'

'So soon?'

'Not soon enough,' Shrikant stared at his table.

Khambe's bushy white eyebrows rose.

'My wife doesn't keep well. I must look after her.'

Khambe nodded sympathetically.

'Dr Sinkar will take over my practice. He's a physician. He won't need a compounder. But I have told him you speak Marathi, Hindi and English. He says he would be happy to employ you as a receptionist. So you still have your job.'

'Receptionist?' Khambe looked doubtful. 'That's a woman's job.'

Shrikant stared at him. Then shrugged.

Khambe hastened to explain. 'When you told me about retiring, I gave my future some thought.' He paused, waiting for Shrikant to prod him further. When Shrikant merely looked, Khambe said, 'I have decided to retire too. I have no responsibilities. My daughter is married. My son has a good job. I long to return to Chiplun to look after the family house.'

'In that case, I will pay you a month's salary as I had said I would. Cash as usual?'

❧

On Shrikant's first day home Gulab said, 'I'm trying to take her to the bathroom. Her legs give way. Can you help me please?'

Shrikant looked at Usha's face as she lay in bed, thin, blank-eyed, blank-faced. Emotion leaves lines on the face like receding waves on sand. Shrikant couldn't remember when he had last seen Usha laugh or weep.

'Let her be,' he said softly. 'We will give her a sponge bath. I will.'

'Let me do it, saheb. It's my job.'

'Thank you, Gulab. I will need your help.'

It became a ritual then. By the time Gulab arrived, Shrikant would have had his morning tea and bath. Gulab would prepare basins of warm water, a solution of mild soap, pads of soft wash towels and large towels to cover and absorb. Shrikant would undress his wife carefully under her sheet. Starting with her face, he would work downwards, meticulously sponging the deep hollows above and below her collarbones, her armpits, under her shrunken breasts, her groin and fastidiously between her toes. 'You have a fetish for toes,' Usha used to say in their early days together.

'Only yours,' he would say. 'They are so perfectly formed and so precisely graded from the big toe to the little toe.'

After the sponge bath, Shrikant sprinkled Usha's back and front liberally with baby powder, buttoned her into a fresh gown, combed her short sparse hair and sighed with profound pleasure. The small of his back hurt. He took the weight off his feet, lowered himself into his chair and put his feet up on the cushioned stool that Gulab brought him.

'You can have your bread and tea now, Gulab,' he said.

'I can have it later, saheb. Your papers are in the hall.'

'Are they? Good. Let them be. Do have your breakfast. I want to spend time talking to my wife. I'll call you when I need you.'

Gulab gave him a look of non-comprehension and left the room.

Shrikant leaned forward and took Usha's thin hand in his and began to speak.

This was to be his life for as long as he had things to say and he could tell himself she was listening. Mornings were the best time to talk. The sponge bath had a calming effect on Usha. You could never be sure about the rest of the day. There were bouts of agitation, accusation, hallucination, all symptoms of time doing its work on her brain. But her mornings were calm. She lay in bed, staring at the ceiling or at a single spot on the wall or sometimes directly at him. She looked fresh. Her wispy hair lifted and fell under the breeze from the fan. The air around her was redolent of baby powder.

'Do you remember how I fell in love with you Usha? At first sight?' he asked, stroking her hand in which the blue veins stood out in a network of rounded ridges. 'I've told you about it a dozen times. Each time I did, you smiled and said, "That's an old story, Shri." But it's still fresh in my mind, my love. It was at Prabha's twenty-first, remember? Our entire gang was there. We were all a little less, a little more than twenty-one. A couple of years away from our degrees. Much was to happen later. The internship, the two-year stint in a rural community—they made us sign bonds—that's where Manohar and Lata fell in love and got married later. Theirs was one of several village marriages. We were away from family. We thought we were doing noble work. The living conditions were dismal but our spirits were high. Mine were not. I kept remembering you at the twenty-first party. I was looking forward to getting my degree. MBBS was all I wanted. I'd had enough of Human Anatomy, Human Microbiology, Human Pathology…It was the wrong attitude for a doctor. But quite honestly there were times when the human body disgusted me. Not so your sister. Prabha found it endlessly fascinating. She wanted to go on.

Shekhar wanted to go on. Senthil wanted to go on. They were all there, remember? At the party?

'I had never danced. Those who had come from Protestant Mission and convent schools knew how. Prabha did. You did. I was from a Marathi medium school. I stuck to my corner watching. My sister Shalini had once told me that my eyes were like Montgomery Clift's. It had gotten me suddenly interested in him. I saw *From Here to Eternity* when it came here. I read up on him. A journalist had once described his eyes as "Large, liquid, pleading". I was testing mine out that evening. Pleading with you to look at me. Perhaps come over. Talk.'

Shrikant looked at Usha's placid face. 'Do you know why I have told you this story so often? Because I hoped to hear you say that you too had loved me the way I loved you. I was so full of doubt.' He paused. 'I'm still in doubt. Did you love me darling? Ever?'

There was a knock at the door. Gulab peeped in. 'Doctor saheb has come.'

Senthil had promised to drop in every morning. Not as a doctor. As a friend. To give Shrikant moral support.

'Is she taking her pills?'

Shrikant shook his head. 'No food either. Holds everything in her mouth. Gulab takes it out.'

'Liquids?'

'Some.'

'Keep giving her that. We don't want her to dehydrate.'

He looked at Shrikant with a neutral face. 'You know we could put in a Ryle's tube and a drip.'

'I know. Tea?'

'No. Hospital rounds. See you tomorrow. Have you been talking to her?'

'Yes. Hasn't worked so far.'

'But you'll keep trying? It'll help you more than her.'

That evening they wheeled Usha to the sit-out. Gulab tied a bib around her neck and went in to fetch tea. The sun was dipping behind the roofs across the road bringing the bare branches of the gulmohar to golden life. Shrikant settled down with his tea next to Usha while Gulab spooned some into Usha's reluctant mouth. He watched her throat closely. He saw no movement. A little while later, the tea which had collected in her mouth dribbled on to her bib.

'Let me try,' he said. 'Here love. Tea from my cup.' He spooned a few drops into her mouth, gently prying it open with the tip of the spoon. 'Remember who gave us this tea-set, darling? It's forty years old. Did you know that, Gulab? We've been married forty years. And look at this cup and saucer. No staining, no chipping.'

'Has she swallowed the tea?' Gulab asked softly.

'I think she has.' Shrikant could not hide his tears. That spoonful was the only liquid Usha had that evening.

'Senthil came yesterday. He'll come again,' Shrikant said as he checked Usha's blood pressure. 'You looked at him. He smiled at you and waved. He said you looked good. He thought you were doing well. Isn't that nice to hear? You saw that, didn't you?'

When Senthil came, Usha was asleep.

'Blood pressure's low,' Shrikant said.

'She looks calm though. No agitation? No restlessness?'

'It starts in the evening. Muttering. Hallucinations.'

'But when you talk?'

'She's calm.'

'I don't have to tell you that…'

'No. She is showing all the classic symptoms—can't swallow. Sleeps most of the time.'

'Watch her breathing.'

'I sleep with my hand on her chest.'

Senthil nodded and left.

'As I was saying, my darling, I was waiting to hear you say you loved me. But you never did.' He thought Usha's hand trembled in his. 'You said I was your best friend, your trusted friend. It made me happy to hear you say that. But not happy enough. I yearned to be more. I yearned for you to have eyes only for me the way I had eyes only for you. But I was prepared to wait. Who knew but I might one day find a way to you. Till then, being your trusted friend, your escort to plays and films and parties was a way to hold on. It was a tie to bind you to me, however loosely, however tenuously.

'Being with you was an education. I saw films I would never have seen, plays I would not even have heard of. One film disturbed me deeply. *Jules et Jim.* What a horrible woman she was and poor Jules, so honest, so loyal. You kept saying what a film, what a film. In the end, I said I hated it. Why, you asked me full of surprise. I was gathering courage to say I hated it because I hated the woman, when you began telling me about the new wave films in France and drifted away from the question you had asked. I want to tell you now, why I hated the film. I hated it because I hated the woman. I was Jules and the woman was you. Yet it wasn't. You weren't like that. You would have been straight with me, wouldn't you? If you couldn't be with me, you would know you couldn't be with me and you would say you couldn't be with me, wouldn't you? Not humiliate me like that woman humiliates Jules.'

Shrikant leaned forward and stroked Usha's face.

'You remember, gamin Usha? That's how Pierre described you. You were offended when I told you. As always, to be with you was both joy and pain. We were at the Alliance remember? To welcome the new director, Pierre Bernoulli. When you showed me the invitation card, I thought with great relief that I'd be able to say both his names unlike the chap at the House of Soviet Culture where we had seen some Russian film and you had introduced him as someone called something with a lot of unpronounceable k's and z's in the name. I was quite jaunty when I came to pick you up. "So off we go to welcome Pierre Bernuli," I said. You laughed delightedly. "Dear dear Shrikant," you said. "You don't do 'r' like a road roller as we do in Marathi. It's guttural. Like this. Piekh Bekhnuyi. Try."

'"You try choledocholithiasis."

'"Touche," you said and squeezed my arm. It stayed squeezed through the night and into the morning. You weren't to know that of course. You were also not to know that for many days after, I went Piekhr, Piekhr, Piekhr in the bathroom assuming the sound of water covered it. But one day Mother passing by said, "Are you ok?" and I said, "Something in the throat. No worries," and carried on soaping my stomach. That day I swore off the Frenchman's name. I decided to be airy and call him PB. The Alliance director before PB had been simple. Antoine Delon. Nothing guttural. Once you knew the "oi" in the first name was "w", Antwan, and the "on" in the last was nasal like in Konkani, you were on easy first and/or second name terms with him.

'But PB stumped me. At one point that evening, he wandered over to me and, looking appreciatively at you, said, "Your wife is, how I say it, gamine." I reported the remark faithfully to you. Well, not quite faithfully. I forgot to mention "wife" though I will say it now. It made me tingle all over. Bless the man. His rule book for foreign cultures must have told him that in India it was best to assume a man and woman together in public were husband and wife. So thorough had his preparation for India been that he had not heard you introduce me to him more pointedly than you needed to as "mon ami Shrikant".

'"He said I was gamine?"

'"Yes."

'"In French?"

'"No no. English."

'"Using the French word?"

'"Which one?"

'"Gamine?"

'"Oh? That's French? Isn't Audrey Hepburn called that? I thought it was very nice. He wasn't being rude, was he?"

'"Not rude to call me a boyish child-woman?" you asked stiffly.

'I kept quiet. Maybe some subtle French line had been crossed that I knew nothing of. There had been no report of Audrey Hepburn being offended. But she was British.'

They sat on the sit-out at tea time every evening. Shrikant loved being there with Usha, Gulab perched on the parapet ready to spring up at a look from him. One evening, as the sun dipped, a dark cloud blotted it. A fresh breeze sprang up, rustling through the trees. A while later, Shrikant heard the unmistakable susurration of rain. The whisper built into a distinct chatter. Large drops of rain formed coronets in the dry mud and a warm smell rose from the earth. The first monsoon rain.

'Can you smell it, Usha? Your favourite fragrance. Sanjeev got you a vial of attar from Kannauj that captured this very scent. Remember?'

Usha laughed. Shrikant looked at her stunned. But then she became agitated.

'Oilcan,' she muttered. She looked at Gulab and shouted 'You stole the oilcan, Mummy!' and struggled to get up. Shrikant held her gently down. Gulab was already up. They wheeled her to the bedroom. She muttered on and on, her voice rising and falling. Shrikant stroked her forehead. 'Yes, my love. Yes.'

She went on about a man looking and a chair and the oilcan and mummy.

Tears trickled down Shrikant's cheeks. Through them he said, 'Gulab, try and give her some milk please. Just warm, all right? I'll call the children.'

❧

In the morning Usha looked perky. She smiled when Shrikant sponged her. 'You like that, don't you?' he asked, happy to see her smile, although she didn't know who she was or who he was, nor could she connect sensation and emotion.

'On peut Paris merci, le la dix son garcon lit…' Usha babbled happily in French all through the sponging.

'Can you turn on your side, love? We'll do your back.' A great frown gathered on her forehead. 'Who?' she said nodding. Then relapsed into silence.

As he powdered her, Shrikant said softly, 'Can I talk to you, my darling? Or does it exhaust you? I have so much to say.'

Usha hummed tunelessly. She could never hold a note. But she knew dozens of songs in English, Marathi, Hindi, French. If that was her mood, he decided to talk about songs.

'Remember the song they played at the Alliance party that made people go misty-eyed? On the way home I asked you about the song. You spoke of Edith Piaf and translated the first few lines of the song for me. I still remember them.

'Beneath the Paris sky / flutters a song / It was born today / in a young man's heart / Beneath the Paris sky / lovers stroll / Happy because the song / is made for them.

'You were soon to go to Paris. You kept repeating the first line of the song—*Sous le ciel de Paris*. And you kept saying "Oh Shri, I am so excited. So excited. Paris. It's like home. A home that was always there, waiting. And now, I'll be there. *Sous le ciel de Paris.*"

'I nodded rather more vigorously than I felt like. I wanted you to know I was happy for you. Such an honour. Working on your thesis in the mother of French universities. The Sorbonne.

'You left. Was this a permanent break? I dared not think it. Then your first letter arrived. Par Avion. Followed by others. A regular stream. Your parents, like mine, were gone. But your sisters were there. You were close to Prabha. I asked her once, do you hear from Usha? She said only once in a while. That seemed odd. I needed to know why I was the chosen one. I didn't need to ask the question. Prabha supplied the answer.

'"Dearest Shri. Don't you know? She can say absolutely anything to you. You never judge her. You never argue."

'"I'm like a wall?"

'"How can you say that?" Prabha was astonished. "She'd be a fool to bounce her ideas off a wall. I don't have your patience. You listen, respond. Come on, Shri. Accept it. You're a good man."

'Why wasn't that enough? Why was I hounded by doubt?

'How could I be your best friend? I a general practitioner, you a brilliant scholar of French, an intellectual! I was so out of my depth with you. What made you write to me about your thesis? I knew it was going to be about some character called Emma Bovary. But she became your obsession. You thought the author was punishing her for dreaming of romance. If he cared for her, he would still punish her but there would be pain in the punishment. What could I say to that? You said a writer should care for all his characters. Look how

Tolstoy treats Anna. She too was an adulteress. She too craved romance. But Tolstoy cared for her. He gave her dignity, wit, elegance. Emma's author made her empty-headed. He made her dreams naive, fatuous.

'It was all gobbledygook to me. But you trusted me with these thoughts. I felt elated. I felt inadequate. I looked up "fatuous". I went to Strand Book Stall and bought a copy of *Madame Bovary*.'

Shrikant got up. There was only one book of fiction among his medical tomes. He fished it out from the back of the shelf. The pages had been crisp when he bought it. They were brittle and yellow now.

'Here it is,' he said returning to his chair. Usha's eyes were closed. That's all right, he thought. I'll show her the book when she wakes up.

'I ploughed through this thing. Did you know that? I had never read a novel before and I haven't read another since. But this thing I ploughed through. It was laborious reading. And deeply painful. I wasn't absorbing anything. I detested Emma because she was being untrue to her husband. She was embracing Rodolphe passionately while Charles Bovary the innocent, the unsuspecting, the general practitioner, was alone at home. I began to see myself in him as I had seen myself in Jules. I marked these lines: *Charles's conversation was commonplace as a street pavement, and everyone's ideas trooped through it in their everyday garb, without exciting emotion, laughter, or thought.*

He had never had the curiosity, he said, while he lived at Rouen, to go to the theatre to see the actors from Paris. That was me. That was bloody me. Why was I pretending to be anything else? Worse. You weren't Emma. You were Anna. Witty, elegant, dignified, but also looking for romance. Living in the city of love. Under the Paris sky where songs are made for lovers.

'I prepared myself for the worst when you started writing about your Russian Jewish friend Yakir Dvorkin. He was so intelligent. A genius in fact. He was this. He was that. Coffee with Yakir in Les Deux Magots where Sartre and Simone de Beauvoir hung out with other intellectuals. Then suddenly you were writing about the workers' and students' revolt. I couldn't see you in that melee. Nor were you. But you wrote about it as excitedly as you had written about Dvorkin. Where did he disappear? You stopped mentioning him. What happened? You never said. But now you were writing about someone called Daniel Cohn-Bendit who had instigated the revolt. You wrote breathlessly about Sartre addressing the students at the Sorbonne. You wrote about police action against students and their arrest. I was worried. Were you going to be arrested? Then came a line in one of your letters, looking back on the revolt. It stunned me with its matter-of-factness. "All that the students at Nanterre University wanted was to sleep with each other," you wrote. But wasn't Nanterre a part of the Sorbonne? So that's what the students of your university wanted? And you thought that was all? Then the dreams began. You and Dvorkin all sweaty in bed. Thank God Mad May was soon over and done with. A year later your thesis was accepted. March 1970 you defended it. July 1970 you were coming home.

'Your last letter from Paris said, "I long to see you again."'

Sleeping beside Usha with his hand on her chest, Shrikant got up with a start. He hadn't felt her breath. He checked her pulse and sighed with relief.

'Very shallow breathing,' he said to Senthil when he came the next day. 'I think she stopped breathing for a few seconds at one point.'

Senthil put his hand on Shrikant's shoulder and squeezed it.

'I was at the airport to receive you that morning. July 22, 1970. Waiting with me was that magical line from your letter causing irrepressible bubbles in the heart. "I long to see you."

'The indicator board had announced that your flight was delayed but not by how long. Doubts began to assail me. Was I waiting for the right flight? Was it coming that day? Or the next? I drew your aerogramme out of my pocket just to check. Checking was merely an excuse. What I wanted was to re-experience the warm notes around the heart that your line played each time I read it. There it was. "I long to see you again." Long? No. Really? Long? Warm notes? I dared not think it.

But yes. It wasn't "I look forward to seeing you again." That would have fitted with "Mon ami Shrikant". But long? That was…that was…Sitting half off the ledge outside Mumbai airport, I allowed myself to smile. I took a last look at the letter before I slipped it back into my pocket. The line hadn't disappeared. It wasn't, "I look forward to seeing you." No. It was still "I long to see you." For the first time since I had read *Madame Bovary*, I felt convinced I was not Dr Charles Bovary, the dull, unambitious, good-hearted doctor. I did not need to fear any Rodolphe Boulanger. Or Leon. Or Dvorkin or whoever else.

'I kept staring at the arrivals board, willing it to change the status of the only flight that existed for me from "Scheduled" to "Arrived". It did that within the few seconds it took me to pull my handkerchief out and dab at my forehead. My heart went into top gear. My eyes were now fixed on the exit gate. Half an hour more of waiting and then I saw you. You were looking out for me. I was waving my hand like a madman gone doubly mad. You spotted me. You quickened your pace. I was overcome by confusion. How to greet you. It had always been just a casual Hi. But now…before I knew the answer, you had flung your arms around me. I was aware that mine were hovering uncertainly six inches away from your back. Then they clasped you for a few brief moments before flying apart. It was all too much for me. I had to quieten my heart, "So how was it? The flight, the flight?" I picked up your suitcases without waiting for an answer and began walking towards the parking lot.

'"Car?" you asked.

'"Borrowed," I replied.

'"I'd have been fine in a cab."

'I muttered something apologetic and smiled to make it positive.

'"How I've longed to see you," you said, your voice sounding wistful. I turned around sharply. Why did you sound wistful? I was there, the man you had been longing to see. You looked at me with a tender smile. "Good old Shrikant," you said. "To know you would still be here. You have no idea what that meant to me in the mad whirl of Paris."

'My heart stopped racing. We were back on track.

'It was a long ride to Colaba to the Women Graduates Hostel. It would take us forty-five minutes to get there. That was forty-five minutes of just you and me I thought. People stared at us along the way. Not because we were we. But because we were in a red MG sportscar.

'"Whose car?"

'"Old friend from college. Comes from Sagar."

'"Are people in Sagar so…?"

'I remember smiling at your suspicious tone. "You think it's stolen? His family are malgujars."

'"What's that?"

'"I don't know. When he told me, he sounded like everybody knew what it was."

'"He loaned it to you? To fetch me? You said to him there's this fancy woman from Paris. I need something flashy to pick her up?"

'There was an edge to your voice but you were also laughing.

"That doesn't sound like me, does it?"

'"H'm. I don't know. People change."

'"Me? Good old Shrikant the constant?"

'"Sorry sorry sorry." You leaned your head on my shoulder. That was lovely.

'"Here's the story," I said. "This fellow, Anil Gupta, has given up engineering. He's gone to FTII. He wants to direct films. Crazy idea. But he's the only son of a rich father. So why not. He's left the car in my care. Because I have a house with space around it where it can be parked safely."

'"And because you will look after it like your own."

'"Good old Shrikant, right?"

'I think I sounded a little bitter. Wrong tone. I had to lighten the mood.

'"Anil is crazy about Rat Pack music. He's had a cassette deck fitted in here. I've been listening to his collection and love it."

'I had already selected the songs I wanted you to hear with me and had put them on a single cassette. I switched on the player. Frank Sinatra's voice came flooding in. *Close to you, I will always stay/Close to you, though you're far away.*

'Then Dean Martin with *When somebody loves you*.

'"Oh, I love that," you said. "What an easy voice he has. Like a cat slipping into bed with you."

'"What a striking description of a voice," I said. "I could never think of saying something like that."

'"But you felt it, Shri. That's the point. We can't all be everything, can we? We can't all have everything, can we? We must see our own limits. Accept them. I could never match up to Yakir. I was always tongue-tied in his presence."

'"You?" I said. But you didn't hear me.

'"Yakir was a Bohemian. Not a pretend one. A genuine one. I wasn't. I pretended. But he could see straight through me. What was the point of it all?"

'I was feeling elated and depressed. With you in the early days it was always that mix of emotions. Your question stuck sharp pins in my heart. "What was the point of it all." What was that "all"? "All" they wanted was to sleep with each other.

'You looked at me. I think you saw the pain in my eyes.

'"Can we stop for a moment, please?"

'We were on Marine Drive. It would have taken us ten minutes to get to the hostel.

'"Aren't you tired?"

'"I am. But I'll be less tired when I get this burden off my chest."

'I stopped the car. My heart was thumping. I knew what was coming.

"Shri, I slept with Yakir. Then I discovered he was sleeping with others."

'I said nothing. The silence was loud. It hummed in my ears. Yours too, I suppose. You gave me time. Then you said, "There are people who cannot be anything but themselves. They wouldn't know how. There aren't many of them. I've met only one. You. There are many more like me. Confused. Unsure. Wanting this. Wanting that. If they are lucky, they live through all of that and still find their way home. I have found mine. Will you marry me, Shri? Please?"

'I looked at you. Your eyes were clear. You knew what you were doing. I knew this was the moment I had longed for but never thought would come. It had come. But the light was obscured by a cloud.

'"You don't have to say either yes or no. I know how you feel. Perhaps I shouldn't have told you. But how could I do that to you? I did so want us to start with a clean slate. I want to say just one thing. There is nothing left of that brief madness. Nothing. You must believe this."'

Shrikant looked at Usha. She was fast asleep.

That night Usha began making a strange noise in the back of her throat. It was like the regular ticking of a clock. Tic. Then a couple of minutes later tic again. Shrikant sat beside her, his hand on her chest. In the morning the rain came down in a sharp shower. It came slamming down, hitting the window pane and dribbling in. He got up to shut the window. The shower wasn't going to last. The tender morning sun was still out, lighting up each needle of water into rainbow colours. He was at the window when the bell rang. He hurried to let Gulab in. When he returned to the room, the ticking in Usha's throat had slowed down. He was back in his chair, his hand on her chest. Gulab stood by looking at Usha and then at him. At one point he took his hand off her chest and leaned back in his chair.

'I'll sponge her,' he said. He did. Then he said, 'Please stay with her. I'll have my bath.'

He did. He came out dressed in a crisp white pajama-kurta.

'Can you leave us alone now please?'

Gulab nodded and tiptoed away. When Senthil came, he asked her, how is she. He saw her face and knew. He knocked on the door. There was no answer. He knocked again. Louder. There was no answer. He pushed the door open. Shrikant lay beside Usha, his hand on her chest. A syringe lay on a side table, an envelope beside it, marked 'Senthil'.

He opened it and read.

Dearest Friend,

I know I have made matters complicated for you. Deal with them as best you can. But this isn't suicide. This is being together. We are on our way home.

Much gratitude,

Shrikant